# THE MEMBRANES

T0049276

# THE MEMBRANES

## A NOVEL

## CHI TA-WEI

TRANSLATED BY

## ARI LARISSA HEINRICH

Columbia University Press    *New York*

Columbia University Press wishes to express its appreciation
for assistance given by the Pushkin Fund
in the publication of this book.
Columbia University Press
*Publishers Since 1893*
New York    Chichester, West Sussex
cup.columbia.edu
Membranes © Ta-Wei Chi 1996, 2011
English edition © Columbia University Press 2021
Originally published in Complex Chinese by
Linking Publishing Co., Ltd., in Taiwan
Published by arrangement with Linking Publishing Co., Ltd.,
through Ailbert Cultural Company Limited
Sponsored by the Ministry of Culture, Republic of China (Taiwan)

Library of Congress Cataloging-in-Publication Data
Names: Ji, Dawei, 1972- author. | Heinrich, Ari Larissa, translator.
Title: The membranes : a novel / Ta-wei Chi ; translated by
Ari Larissa Heinrich.
Other titles: Mo. English
Description: New York : Columbia University Press, [2021] |
Series: Modern Chinese literature from Taiwan
Identifiers: LCCN 2020045603 (print) | LCCN 2020045604 (ebook) |
ISBN 9780231195706 (hardback) | ISBN 9780231195713 (trade paperback) |
ISBN 9780231551441 (ebook)
Classification: LCC PL2842.D39 M62513 2021  (print) |
LCC PL2842.D39 (ebook) | DDC 895.13/6—dc23
LC record available at https://lccn.loc.gov/2020045603
LC ebook record available at https://lccn.loc.gov/2020045604

Cover design: Julia Kushnirsky
Cover photograph: Kateryna Bibro / Alamy Stock Photo

# CONTENTS

# THE MEMBRANES

# 1

omo brushed her yellow bedroom wallpaper with her fingers. Then she bit gently into a hothouse peach, sweet juice oozing from pink skin so delicate it would bruise if you blew on it. Had she perceived the yellow paper through direct exposure to her subcutaneous neural network? Was it her taste buds that detected peach sweetness? She would never know. An impenetrable barrier existed between her body and the material world.

Membranes filtered Momo's every impression of the world. At thirty, she felt there was at least one layer of membrane between her and the world. Not the kind of membrane she applied to her clients receiving facials at work, obviously. The invisible kind. The kind that made her feel sort of like a tiny water flea—a *Daphnia* encased in a cell, swimming alone out to sea. The ocean surrounded her body but never touched her.

Momo was a kind of aesthetician known as a "dermal care technician." She knew that between her clients' faces and her own hands—beyond the seaweed and the carmine masks—lay another membrane that prevented her from ever truly getting close to anyone. Momo was acutely unsuited to intimacy. People who didn't know her often found her reticence alluring; her regulars just assumed she was the quiet type.

Unsuited? More like suspended in an amniotic sac. Momo was vaguely aware that she would never fit in here. Sometimes she wondered if she should even be living in this world. Not that she wanted to die. It was just that maybe she was better suited to another space, another world: a misfit peach, unsatisfied with its home tree and dreaming of growing on a different tree.

But isn't one peach tree the same as any other?

No.

Two peach trees, two entirely different universes.

Momo's fate began with peaches. For as long as she could remember, their sweetness warmed her. Just a morsel in her mouth transported her back to her fairy-tale youth. All through those ten long, hard years spent studying at boarding school, before bed she would relish the taste of a luscious hothouse peach, nourishing her body while also rewarding herself after an arduous day, sending herself off to sweet peachy dreams. Though her reticence kept people from getting close to her, anyone would agree that this peach-loving girl—with her blushing white face—was herself as sweet as a peach. Even her name. Momo. Somewhere between a murmur and the Japanese word for "peach."

Once, little Momo asked her mother, "Where did I come from?"

"You weren't born from a womb," said her mother, "and you weren't plucked from a trash heap."

What Momo's mother told her next was not the simple, perfunctory version of what you learn in sex ed. Instead she explained that a long, long time ago, Mommy had taken a trip with a friend.

They were walking along hand in hand in the hills when they came to the base of a peach tree at the top of a knoll. The peaches gave off a mesmerizing scent: to smell them was to go limp with ecstasy. Not worrying about pesticides or being accused of theft, Mommy's friend asked Mommy to let her stand on her shoulders. With a little teamwork, the crafty pair plucked the biggest peach of all. It was as big as a human head. Mommy was delighted. She told her friend: "In China there's a legend that 'peach splitting'—when you share a peach with a friend—is the mark of an extraordinary friendship, the kind that other people wouldn't understand. Let's share the peach and bless our friendship!" And so, according to Momo's mother's story, the two women split the peach with a knife . . . never anticipating that, as soon as the knife broke the skin, a shrill wailing cry would burst out of the peach. Inside was a baby! As shocked as they were, both women felt that this tiny baby was destined to be their daughter. It was just like a fairy tale.

The baby's face was bright red and sweetly fragrant. A peach child. Mommy's friend explained that according to an ancient Japanese legend, there was once a little boy who had been born from a peach, and his name was Momotaro the Peach Boy. Since "Peach" was pronounced "Momo" in Japanese, it was decided: she would be Momo.

"And that's where you came from," said Momo's mother.

To little Momo this story sounded bizarre. It was the twenty-second century, and Momo had a basic understanding of sex. But she liked that it was at least unique. So . . . why not choose to believe it? Momo took a certain pride in the romance of her genesis.

But in that case, Momo wondered, where was Mother's Japanese friend now? Who was she? And why hadn't Momo ever met her?

Momo's mother was evasive. "We had a fight," she said. "Friends fight and break up sometimes; it happens all the time. So that's why Mommy was left to take care of you by herself."

Little Momo thought: *When I grow up, I'll never fight with my friends. I'll be close with my friends forever.*

Forever. Yes, forever.


Thirty-year-old Momo fondled the sweet peach, as soft and delicate as a breast.

Momo and her mother hadn't seen each other in twenty years. Was it even necessary? They'd been estranged for so long that the relationship was now beyond repair, and they'd been reduced to polite, impersonal exchanges.

Was her mother even curious about her?

Momo didn't want to admit it, but she was curious about who her mother had become.

Holding the peach, Momo studied the brand new middle finger of her right hand, thinking of her recent minor surgery. The finger worked perfectly.

Before the surgery, she had begun to feel the occasional prickle in her hand. It wasn't agile the way she needed. After a screening by the Automatic Community Health System, she discovered that her middle finger had been suffering from a kind of occupational health injury. It would be necessary to replace the finger with a custom transplant. The procedure was entirely automated.

Momo hated surgeries. Especially automated surgeries. She would erase all memory of them if she could. But for the sake of her career she had no choice but to replace the finger.

A finger transplant surgery wasn't expensive. And the process was not especially inconvenient or painful: you just went to the appointed window at the hospital, stuck your finger in, and waited while a mold was created. The next day, you returned to the same window and received a local anesthetic. Half an hour later the hospital installed the appropriate spare part. Then you just rested for an hour until your blood circulation returned to normal, and it was business as usual.

Did Momo hate the idea of finger transplant surgery because she worried about damaging her reputation? That wasn't it. As with a pianist, her professional excellence, and her celebrity, ultimately depended on her fingers. Momo's clients were her piano, and her skillful fingers could salvage the worst musical composition. If people in the industry found out about the surgery, they would just love to see her slip up. And if her clients found out, they might question her work. But Momo paid no mind to any of this. In fact, she personally volunteered news about her surgery to the media without regard for her professional standing. She had absolute confidence that her craftsmanship would make up for any deficiency in her hand.

So Momo's anxieties about the surgery didn't stem from any fears about her reputation. That wasn't it.

She simply detested anything to do with surgery.

Momo pressed a key on the remote control and a panel above her head opened, revealing the membrane above, the liquid sky.

Momo's salon was located in a swanky residential community, so the membrane in the air above it was mostly clear of barnacles like sea anemones or coral obscuring the view. With a tilt of her head, Momo could watch the ceaseless crash and break of the silver-indigo waves in the infinite depth beyond the protective membrane and the schools of cadmium yellow fish floating by in tidy regiments.

Just then a black shadow darted swiftly across the waves. Her head resting in her hands, Momo thought it must be an MM, amphibious snipers that could also go on land. She'd heard there was still some military turmoil up there, so it wasn't surprising to see the occasional guerilla MM flitting across the sea.

When Momo was little, she had wanted to go up above the water and get a look at the surface world. She never realized her dream because the law stipulated that only adults could go up to the surface. By the time she was thirty years old, Momo had made her peace with staying put in a corner of the city beneath the ocean. She no longer felt any pressing desire to go sightseeing on the surface; she would never set foot on the land she'd fantasized about a million miles above. How curious she had been about the surface world back then!

She took a big bite out of the peach, chewing slowly.

She fell asleep, and the peach pit rolled out of her hand.

She dreamed that she was living on the surface, and an ear-splitting static penetrated her whole body, which was flat like a fish. She was naked in the white-hot sunlight, and the ultraviolet rays pierced the pores in the membrane of her fragile, realistic skin. And there was nothing she could do about it.

Such were the nightmares of the denizens of the ocean floor in the summer of the year 2100.

# 2

Under the shimmering skylight, Tomie stretched out on the massage table in front of Momo, completely naked. Fresh from Momo's massage, the white of the skin of Tomie's back refracted a healthy rose glow. Cherry blossoms embroidered on silk. Though Tomie was over fifty years old, her body had a severe, uncompromising beauty—due of course to Momo's exceptional skill.

Momo never imagined that Tomie would actually bring over the dog she'd been telling her about. A several-week-old ball of fluff the color of rice, with a pair of gleaming oil-black eyes peering out. Tomie knew full well that Momo preferred the peace and quiet of being on her own, but she brought the dog over anyway, and didn't worry about whether Momo would be angry.

"Momo! This dog is absolutely not your ordinary, everyday pet! It's an extraordinary pet for an uncommon person. And forget the story I told you last time. This little pup is very quiet. You don't have to worry that he'll make lots of noise."

Momo didn't refuse.

"Momo! What will you call him?" Tomie asked.

"I'll call him Andy," Momo replied.

"Momo, don't joke, this is a real live dog, this is no android dog. How can you call it that?"

"But I like the name Andy."

Tomie Ito was Japanese. A regular client of Momo's, she came to the salon for tune-ups. Tomie was sexy. She was a keen-witted and capable disczine reporter stationed in Taiwan who had a knack for unearthing sensational inside stories that earned her a fair bit of money under the table. Momo's services didn't come cheap, so her clients were typically well-heeled consumers with deep pockets.

Momo was introverted by nature but inevitably had intimate contact with her clients. She'd hung out her shop sign at twenty, and when at thirty she'd saved enough money, she purchased a small, quiet live-work salon that consisted of two main structures joined in the shape of an infinity symbol. Now Momo only worked with existing clients and only took advance bookings. For all communications including bookings, she required her clients to use the old-fashioned format of e-mail. Momo believed writing a note was cleaner and more peaceful in the end. Most of all, she hated video calls; they were noisy, an invasion of privacy, and Momo especially loathed getting a phone call when she was in the shower. Did they really expect her to come running for the phone with her bare ass hanging out?

Momo was accustomed to a simple life. She preferred writing letters to talking on the phone. She also didn't go out much; it was enough to watch the news online. Using the Gopher system was more convenient than flipping through a newspaper anyway. And if she wanted to buy anything, she just ordered it online—no need to go out. Her body hadn't changed much over the years, so it wasn't like she needed the gym—and she had no interest whatsoever in the pick-up scene there. So she lived in total solitude in her infinity-shaped house. Occasionally she'd put on arias by the famous *castrato* Farinelli.

Like her name implied, Momo's personality was quiet as a murmur, but her reputation was hardly soft-spoken: she was the top skin-care specialist in T City and the city's most respected stylist. Youthful and talented, to the outside world she had a quietly enigmatic presence, quite unlike other, more peacocklike members of her profession.

And it was precisely this enigmatic quality of Momo's that Tomie had banked on in making her own hefty income. The return on her investment in skin care had been significant. Not so long ago, Tomie had come up with the idea for a "Mother's Day" report for a disczine. The subject was simple, clichéd: "Mom and Me." Tomie's colleagues were secretly thrilled about this, since they thought that Tomie Ito must have lost her touch and finally run out of ideas or she wouldn't have come up with such a bland topic. Imagine their surprise when that issue sold like crazy. Older readers bought it for the wistful pleasure of recalling family affection while younger readers found it novel and curious, for nostalgia is often popular; advertising revenue for that issue of the disczine increased by 119 percent. But the article's greatest selling point by far was the special interviews section.

Tomie had taken advantage of their personal relationship to convince Momo—who had never agreed to an interview before—to talk about her own mother. Just imagine: in an era that overvalued corporeal and intellectual "cosmetics" (a.k.a. not just physical beauty but reading disczines), to have the most enigmatic skin-care specialist in T City discuss her relationship with her famous mother—who happened to be the director of public relations for MegaHard Publishing! How apt and moving an interview that would make!

In the original interview, Momo spoke indifferently with Tomie, narrating disparate fragments of her memories and mentioning her recent transplant procedure, utterly unperturbed that her clients might refuse to patronize her salon once they found out she had replaced a finger. But when Tomie assembled these fragments into a narrative, the interview suddenly brimmed with a daughter's yearning for—and resentment of—her successful mother. In this account, Momo's mother came across as stone cold; she knew full well that her daughter had undergone a critical finger transplant that could jeopardize her job and had not even asked how she was.

This issue of the disczine, along with Momo's interview, set everyone buzzing. Momo read the two new BBS e-reports that appeared on her computer screen: one was about the "Find Your Mother" craze that had been set off by the magazine, while the other consisted of some brutally cynical critiques. On BBS, people pointed out how the disczine had exposed some of society's shameful hypocrisies, a case in point being Mega-Hard's director of public relations: she cashed in on her image as a respectable, sweet, and motherly figure, while in real life neglecting her only daughter. The Public Relations Department of MegaHard was obliged to issue a formal letter of clarification over BBS, saying there had been a misunderstanding, and imploring consumers to keep their faith in MegaHard. Momo read it with cold detachment, determined to keep her distance.

"I'm never doing an interview again," she now complained to Tomie, upset that she'd let herself be manipulated. "Whatever happens, please don't leak my e-mail address to reporters. I don't want to see the ranting e-mails from fired-up readers flooding my inbox."

Momo's fingers danced deftly about, her new middle finger moving in harmony without hindering her work in the slightest.

"Mother and I have nothing left to say to each other."

On Tomie's last visit, she had told Momo the story about the dog. Clients always loved to talk to Momo, not just because they felt that Momo was a good listener but because Momo didn't talk much, so she wasn't likely to spread gossip to other clients. Momo's clients included all kinds of celebrities from government, business, cultural, and art circles. They were men and women of all ages, all VIPs. Each of them was vain enough to want to be the topic of conversation, but each was also terrified of someone talking about them in less than glowing terms.

Tomie had gossiped with Momo about all sorts of trade secrets from the world outside, never once worrying that Momo would jeopardize them. But what Tomie mentioned this time wasn't the kind of intelligence you could sell. It was just a trivial matter from her own life.

Tomie told Momo how she'd spent good money to buy a real, live pet dog. Even a mutt cost a bundle. The mutt Tomie bought had a shy disposition; she loved to hide in the crawl space, between the floorboards of Tomie's Japanese-style house and the layer of gingko leaves that covered the ground underneath. When the dog became pregnant, she preferred to stay under there and hardly ever emerged, only showing her face to eat or drink or shit. So one day when Tomie was eating a block of sweet, dense Yokan and sipping some matcha, she realized with a start that it had been a while since she'd seen the dog; she was possibly stuck beneath the floorboards, and worse, Tomie thought she detected the smell of blood wafting up from there. She promptly pried open the flooring, and what she saw nearly made her faint:

orbs of flesh lying like inguinal polyps, ulcers in a pond of purplish-black blood! Turned out the dog had given birth in the crawl space, but was too spent to climb back out afterward. Hungry and tired, she just curled up in the crawl space to await rescue. Previously, Tomie took pride in knowing a thing or two of the world's ruthless grotesquery. She never imagined how shocking she'd find the scene before her. For a moment she was paralyzed with horror.

Tomie forced herself to relax and look at the little balls of flesh pooled in blood. There were six puppies altogether. Tomie was no veterinarian and had no clue how to deliver them; all she could do was look for a pair of scissors. She cut the umbilical cord between the dog and her puppies as blood spurted everywhere. Tomie pulled the mother dog out from the beneath the floorboards and fed her and washed her. But what was she supposed to do with the little balls of flesh that she'd cut free? Each of them was covered in a thin membrane.

Should she cut the membranes open? Tomie wasn't sure. Might as well give it a try. She cut open three of them and left the other three encased in their filmy sheaths. The whole exercise left Tomie's body smeared in blood, and she was so tired and grossed out that she wanted to vomit. So she threw all six balls of flesh into the trash can and closed the lid, too annoyed to think much of it. Then she ran a bath and got in bed.

"Guess what happened next?" Tomie asked Momo.

In the middle of the night, Tomie was woken up by faint but incessant whining sounds. She followed the sounds out to the trash can, where she discovered that the source of the whining was the three hungry puppies that she'd cut from the placental sacs. The other three puppies, trapped in their sacs, had suffocated.

"Momo, at the time I thought there was something poetic about it. It reminded me of something a monk from ancient times once said: 'Grieve, rejoice, give, and receive.' I didn't mourn the loss of three extremely valuable puppies, but neither did I celebrate the fact that I now had three extremely valuable puppies. I didn't grieve, but I didn't rejoice . . ."

"The dead puppies left perfectly intact inside the membrane weren't necessarily more pathetic than the ones that squirmed their way out of the membrane," said Momo.

"Exactly! I raised them and had them all neutered. They're really cute, and they're not noisy—Can I give you one, Momo?"

"Don't even think about it. You've caused me enough trouble."

"I'm not asking you to buy one. It's a gift. This is no man-made android dog—it's a living, breathing mutt. It's worth a lot of money, a lot more than some twentieth-century mongrel. Yes, it's real and it shits. It won't be as clean as an android dog. But it's not every year that you get to catch a whiff of real dog shit." Tomie arched her nose for dramatic flair and added, "There's a little rice-colored puppy that's actually not at all noisy and not naughty. It would be easy to take care of. I'll give you that one."

"Why would you give it to me?" Momo asked.

"It pierced the membrane. It reminds me of you." Tomie's expression was hard to read. "Momo, you're like a freak walled off by membranes and clinging desperately to your routines! Living here all alone in your salon, no assistant, no romance. . . . You never go out, you don't even have a sex life—it's pathetic. Take the puppy. I mean well. I don't have ulterior motives. Besides, you told me yourself you had a serious illness and sick people shouldn't be alone. A puppy to keep you company will be good for you. And a puppy is a simple and easygoing creature . . . not at all like a human."

"Tomie, it was only a minor procedure, and it was successful. Don't make me out to be terminally ill." Momo wasn't used to talking about private things. "Now, Tomie, what shall we do with your skin today?"

"Momo, don't be so stubborn. Next time I'm bringing you the puppy."

Momo worked over every inch of Tomie's body with her fingers, massaging and relaxing the muscles. Then she slathered her in a special emulsion, almost like a peel, since it allowed Momo to peel away the layer of special protective M skin that coated Tomie's body.

All of Momo's clients got "membrane skin" treatments before getting dressed to leave. This was a specialty of Momo's dermal care salon, something only she offered.

Membrane skin, or M skin, was a second skin, literally, that looked no different than face cream, except, when applied, M skin formed a layer of protective membrane over the entire body. It was a bit like applying lacquer to wooden furniture or brushing egg white on pastry, but there was also a more metaphysical aspect to it. A naked body coated in membrane skin had extra luster, and the treatment could help prevent wrinkles by maintaining the right level of elasticity; when you went outside it could also protect against the assault of atmospheric toxins. The high-density biochemical nutritional structure of the membrane-like coating also provided twenty-four-hour protection for the wearer's skin.

Furthermore, as implied by the "skin" part of the name "membrane skin," it was actually just like real skin. Some clients mistakenly believed that the English name M skin stood for "Moreskin," as in, "one MORE layer of skin." But M skin wasn't just some ordinary skin-care emulsion. When you applied M skin, neither water nor sweat, nor alcohol could rub it off. Weeks of vigorous daily lovemaking wouldn't wear it off. The only thing that could remove M skin from the real skin beneath it was Momo's special concoction. Applying M skin caused her clients no discomfort; it was as insubstantial as an odorless perfume, so much so that many clients forgot that there was another, artificial layer of skin on top of their own. Just as well, as long as Momo periodically installed a fresh one.

Momo painstakingly peeled the layer of M skin from between Tomie's legs.

She wouldn't risk painfully yanking Tomie's pubic hair, for Momo, like M skin itself, was soft and forgiving. Once she had peeled off the old layer of M-skin, Tomie's naked body was once again directly exposed to the air. But Tomie was oblivious to this: M skin was so subtle that people couldn't tell when they had it on and when they did not.

Momo placed the M skin *exuviae* carefully into a cellophane bag, which she then filed carefully in one of the small silvery-black drawers of her cabinet.

"Momo? How come you are so fastidious with used M skin?"

"For recycling," Momo said, glancing at Tomie. "The materials aren't exactly cheap. So they have to be recycled. That's why."

In the twentieth century the word "recycling" may have sounded progressive or trendy, but in the bleak desolation of the twenty-second century there was no alternative.

People still said that the natural resources of the oceans were abundant—and they were abundant. But turning the ocean's resources into something humans could actually *use* wasn't exactly convenient.

Or at least, it wasn't as convenient as it had been when people still lived on land.

# 3

It was difficult for late twenty-first-century humanity, living at the bottom of the sea, to imagine life before. The hardest thing to imagine was that some twentieth-century elites actually roasted their skin to the color of burnished copper and considered this hazardous activity a form of leisure!

As terrifying as the sunlight was, and even though the water and air were polluted, still these were the elemental things needed by the denizens of the bottom of the ocean—and they were easier to source aboveground. Solar power especially, which had to be harvested on the surface and then converted for use by the inhabitants below.

Prior to the twenty-first century, humans could still find wild peaches aboveground to pick at will; but by the twenty-first century, peaches—like other fruits and vegetables—had to be cultivated in the greenhouses at the bottom of the ocean. Maintaining these greenhouses—which preserved the remains of humanity—called for vast amounts of sunlight, huge reserves of fresh water, massive volumes of fresh air, and horticultural adaptations—all of which in turn required high degrees of specialized knowledge.

\* \* \*

In the late twentieth century, starting in the 1980s, people discovered the ozone hole—and with the atmosphere's ability to
filter out the sun's harmful ultraviolet rays compromised, inci-
dences of skin cancer skyrocketed. Suntanning not only fell out
of fashion, it became a kind of joke. Now sunglasses were used
for their original purpose instead of for looking cool or hiding
behind.

The scientific community began to call on people to prohibit
the use of fluorocarbons and other chemical compounds that
could further destroy the ozone layer, but scientists knew it was
already too late. Even if humankind succeeded in reducing air
pollution, it would still only slow down—not halt—the inexo-
rable destruction of the environment. Humanity's bad habits
were too deeply entrenched; the time had passed to fix the hole
in the ozone layer.

As the ozone layer deteriorated, ultraviolet rays intensified,
and by the beginning of the twenty-first century, total deaths
from skin cancer eclipsed deaths from other types of cancer,
blood disorders, and neurovascular conditions combined. After
the universal success of the AIDS vaccine in 2009, the terror previously reserved for AIDS now shifted onto the myriad of skin
diseases sweeping the globe.

Even layers of fabric couldn't protect you from the cruelty of
the sun's rays anymore. Only exorbitantly expensive and cumbersome space suits could—the kind astronauts wore, not the
gaudy, popular variety you could pick up for NTD$300 at whole-
sale outlets in the old days. People of all different colors experienced heliophobia, but Black skin provided an extra measure of
protection over white skin, with the result that many white people exchanged their long-standing racism for an open envy of
Black superiority.

Starting in 2010, race-related and sunlight-related tensions in the United States began to coincide. In 2012 alone, Los Angeles experienced sixty-nine separate race riots larger than a hundred, mainly instigated by white people against Black. The whites were upset that their rates of skin cancer were disproportionately higher, which they interpreted as a sign that God had finally shown favor to people of color and scorned white people after all. A number of religions made membership exclusive to people of color—including Christianity, the Yiguan Dao sect, Zorastrianism, Hinduism, Voodoo practices, and Egyptian Revivalism (ancient Egyptians were, after all, Black Africans). Far and wide they proclaimed their gospel: the Creator was not white, but Black. So if white people suffered from a greater proportion of skin cancers, it was just divine retribution for millennia of racial prejudice. Many Native Americans and Asian Americans concurred.

Regardless, Christianity was still the most powerful religion in America, and many Christians—regardless of race—argued that the excess of ultraviolet rays was the second biblical flood: like floodwaters, ultraviolet rays touched every inch of the earth and fell upon the back of every living creature. Humanity needed a refuge. Adapting buildings and making better clothing would never fully solve the problem of exposure, leaders argued. Plus, plants and animals were also exposed to ultraviolet radiation (though they prioritized plants and animals of greatest economic significance for humans, such as livestock, agriculture, tropical horticulture, and so on; other forms of flora and fauna suddenly faded in importance). According to the tenets of Christianity, ancient humans only survived the first great flood because they had Noah's ark; to face ultraviolet radiation, they needed a new ark.

But where and what was it?

Various governments and trusts wanted to become the next Noah. Thanks to advancements in twenty-first-century intelligence and spy networks, classified information now flowed freely among global political and commercial interests, like ghosts passing through a wall. This transparency enabled global VIPs from both government and industry to cooperate openly. And they all reached the same conclusion: there needed to be a massive migration of humankind—plants and animals, accompanied by their respective stewards, naturally—on an unprecedented scale, paralleled only by the great ice age evacuation of the dinosaurs.

These global VIPs also recalled the submerged utopia of Atlantis. Many had seen the classic James Bond film *City Beneath the Sea*, also known in English as *The Spy Who Loved Me*.

Where was the ark? The answer was right in front of them.

It was at the bottom of the sea.

The ocean made a perfect protective membrane, a thick, robust barrier that could shield humans, animals, and plants from ultraviolet radiation.

Plus, the ocean was the primordial birthplace of all earth's plants and animals. Back when there was no life on land, it was the ocean that generated the earliest vegetation, and the ocean that eventually produced our most primitive ancestors. These earliest plants and animals evolved in water because sunlight was lethal; the ozone layer had not yet formed. Only when the collective gases exhaled by the denizens of the ocean had reached a critical mass and erupted through the surface and into the atmosphere was the radiation-filtering protective layer formed. And only under the shelter of this newly formed barrier could the first brave organisms crawl to the shore and withstand the assault of sunlight on their vulnerable bodies.

Who could have imagined that eons later, in the twenty-first century, they would return to their old ocean home?

But humans, unlike fish or shrimp, were not designed to swim, so it would be necessary to build subaquatic cities. Fortunately, the ocean was abundant with natural resources, and with the right adjustments the sea floor could be adapted for human habitation. Not only that, but the technology for harnessing solar power was improving by the day and could now be used to convert great quantities of energy collected aboveground for use on the ocean floor. Since the sun had forced humanity back into the ocean, it was only fair that humanity took some of its power in return.

By the middle of the twenty-first century there was little habitable land left, and humankind finally invaded the oceans en masse, a process euphemistically referred to as "migration." During the process of "reclaiming wasteland," new reserves of crude oil were discovered one after another. This accelerated the rate of underwater construction, which in turn provided a solution to the problem of high unemployment, a surprise benefit of migration to the ocean floor! With great "humanity," they told themselves, humankind "rescued" all manner of favored flora and fauna by bringing them along to the bottom of the sea. This time, of course, they made sure not to bring cockroaches and mosquitos, but they also left behind many critical organisms. Waves of human settlers inevitably led to the ecological devastation of the ocean floor, but people felt they'd done their best to act humanely. *Don't blame us*, they thought, *we did the best we could.*

By 2060, the majority of humanity had migrated to the ocean, with only one percent left to eke out a living on the surface. Pretty much all the main infrastructure of human civilization had migrated to the ocean floor, including industrial agriculture and animal husbandry. All that remained

aboveground were those historical sites too large to be moved—
the pyramids, for example, or the February 28th Incident
Memorial Plaques ubiquitous on the island of Taiwan—though
archeologists and tourists still visited the surface. The new sea
dwellers also left behind unwanted structures like pollution-
producing factories and nuclear power plants (which meant,
however, that some key personnel were forced to remain on the
surface to man the reactors). Also abandoned were prisons and
various tools of punishment, since governments universally
recognized that leaving convicts on the surface was actually a
convenient punishment in and of itself. (Let them burn—who
needed the electric chair!)

The earth's surface, which had once struggled to bear
the burden of overpopulation, was now almost completely
deserted. Though even now humankind proved reluctant to
surrender the legacy of its battles for power, still everything—
everything—on the surface of the earth went the way of the
Great Wall of China. To think that these ambitious marvels of
engineering, built on the backs of the common people, wound
up the playthings of the tourism industry! Their majesty was
reduced to an absurd footnote.

But new, man-made landscapes were also propagated on
the surface. These new landscapes would have been inconceiv-
able to the people who came before: more extravagant than
works by the twentieth-century environmental artist Christo,
but also more practical. For example, there were the metasta-
sizing "fields" of solar panel arrays stretching as far as the eye
could see, used to harvest solar power for the population under
the ocean.

In addition to these solar "fields," a number of new industries
sprang up on the surface, including, most notably, cyborg
factories.

In simple terms, a cyborg was a product that lay somewhere between a human and a robot. You could call it half human and half machine: although its exterior looked strikingly human, it could withstand high temperatures and long exposure to direct sunlight without consequence, and it could work as hard as a machine. While androids and robots were manufactured for hard labor, cyborgs—like humans—were capable of intricate detail work. As a result, cyborgs could replace humans in producing fine handicrafts; they had better dexterity than robots and were more productive than humans. And cyborgs were capable of basic learning and thinking. Being so convenient to use, they were readily adopted both on the surface and on the ocean floor.

Aboveground, cyborgs replaced humans for all work that didn't require complex decision making: they were prison workers, janitors, ticket takers at ancient monuments, workers in factories with elevated levels of pollution, shuttle drivers working between the surface and the ocean floor. . . . Cyborgs kept things on the surface from grinding to a halt. Where human laborers risked sun exposure, cyborgs took their place. Cyborgs also inhabited the cities on the ocean floor, but nobody considered them human: they weren't citizens and had no rights. Incapable of reproducing, they were seen as products—serial numbers and all. And yet cyborgs had much in common with humans: though they possessed far more stamina, their internal organs were structurally analogous. Which was why cyborgs were also considered to be the ideal organ donors. With a cyborg donor, humans didn't have to wait until the donor's brain death before undergoing a transplant surgery. You could sidestep the legal hassles and all those annoying questions of human dignity.

Yet the greatest demand for cyborgs came not from hospitals that performed organ transplants but from the military. Cyborg factories worked hard to keep up with demand, especially for M units.

M units were cyborgs capable of voluntary movement and carrying humans. In the middle of the twenty-first century they were specialized for use in transport, but by 2075, as anticipated, major corporations and world leaders also deployed them for guerilla warfare. Full-scale war was no longer waged by the mid-twenty-first century. But guerilla warfare flourished both on the surface and under the ocean. There were still so many things left to fight over.

As humanity labored to carve out a home in the sea, it seemed to fall right back into colonial ways. In the spirit of progress, corporations and nations alike devised ever more ingenious defense systems. As the world's surface grew increasingly desolate, the various nations deployed standing militias lest anyone seize a piece of their land when they weren't looking. And on the occupied territory of the ocean floor, military powers were even more anxious to hold ground. It had been a free-for-all, initially, as each nation scrambled to claim its turf by sheer force. Luckily in 2079 the New San Francisco Accord (signed in the new, underwater San Francisco) stipulated that the new undersea territories would be distributed based on proportional equivalents to nations' holdings on the surface. This new policy seemed to address each nation's appetite for property, and each country eventually relaxed its initial buffet-style power grab.

The term "buffet" originally described a kind of European culinary tradition in which you could have "all you can eat," dine until your belly was full—but eat too much and you'd get diarrhea. Historians later applied the term metaphorically to the twenty-first-century expansion into ocean territories. The "proportion principle" arrived at was not based on population size or geographic area of land occupied prior to the great ocean migration, but was rather determined by a nation's relative political, economic, and military power. Although France had previously occupied territory smaller than the size of Algeria, the undersea New France occupied six times the size of undersea New Algeria. A full three quarters of the vast Pacific Ocean territories was therefore distributed among only the United States, Japan, and China—while the remaining quarter went mainly to Panasonic, Mitsubishi, Toyota, Formosa Plastics, and Nintendo. The multitude of small island kingdoms of the Pacific were obliged to preserve their tiny footprint when they moved to the ocean floor.

And New Taiwan? While its Pacific territory allotment was hardly satisfactory in size, it was the envy of the rest of the South China Sea. New Taiwan established itself as the financial center of (undersea) Southeast Asia, a key player with unrivaled regional influence.

Developments like these were the product of countless battles, military and otherwise. Yet it seemed that the previous century's nightmare of war still left humanity with less of an appetite for bloodshed in the beautiful new world they'd established on the ocean floor. Let everything ugly and evil be scorched by the sun above. The New San Francisco Accord stipulated that armed conflict was prohibited under the sea; instead it must take place in designated theaters of war on the surface. Consequently a brand-new kind of warfare materialized, featuring fighters who spilled no blood: the insensate M units. Humans were safe and free beneath the ocean—civilized, enlightened—and they could watch the spectacular unending carnage of gladiators battling in barren hellscapes through a variety of electronic devices. It was like watching Nintendo, only the stakes were real. The fate of each and every spectator depended on the outcome.

Safe under the purple sky of a waterproof and earthquake-proof membrane, deep beneath the ocean, people lived out their days like flowers in a greenhouse.

But of course people are not flowers.

Although they were physically removed from the realities of war, they were suspended in a state of virtual escape.

And it felt real to them.

# 4

Little Andy the dog lay obediently at Momo's feet. She turned on her computer routinely to check for bookings.

An unexpected e-mail appeared.

And it wasn't from a client.

Momo required her clients to format their e-mails in a particular way. She tried to avoid the constant stream of spam cluttering the inbox, like the midnight robocalls that plagued the late twentieth century. Momo cursed under her breath. It was probably related to the controversy surrounding Tomie's special feature. Some jerk must have tracked down Momo's e-mail address and was now harassing her in her own home.

But instead of deleting the message, she opened it, skimmed it . . . and was caught off guard. Well, maybe not totally off guard. Momo had been expecting an e-mail like this for a long time.

She just wasn't prepared for it to materialize so suddenly.

## NEW TAIWANNET, E-MAIL BOX

TO: MOMO.BBS@NEW-TAIWAN.NEW-ASIA.
EARTH.SOLAR
FROM: PRESIDENT.BBS@SALES.MEGAHARD.
EARTH.SOLAR

MOMO:

I heard about your recent surgery. I'm worried about you. I'm sorry I can't come see you in person. I also heard that your finger transplant hasn't affected your work at all, and I'm so happy for you. When you were little and sick in the hospital, I wanted to be there with you so much! It's going to be your thirtieth birthday soon, right? We haven't seen each other in twenty years. We really should meet, and luckily I have more free time these days. Please don't be angry that Mommy hasn't been able to be with you. Things have been so hard these twenty years! Write back and tell me when you're available and I'll come see you, okay?

Mommy.
05-05-2100, 11:59 P.M.

PLEASE CHOOSE: (R) REPLY, (C) CANCEL,
(E) EXIT

Should she press "R" and reply?
Or "C" and delete it?
Or "E," as if it were nothing special?
She would select C or E, she figured. But when her computer flashed to the next screen, she found she had clicked R.

Why had her mother written now? In the magazine interview, Momo had complained that Mother had neglected her daughter, which in turn led readers to question the sincerity of one of MegaHard's chief executives. Why press this tidy and awkward letter into Momo's hand now? Mother wrote that she had "more free time these days." Didn't she mean that MegaHard had forced her to take a leave of absence in an effort to do damage control on her image? Mother could come see Momo now? Momo's successful surgery was a long time ago!

But Momo didn't write about her suspicions, or her feelings of resentment.

She just typed out a date when they could meet.

Might as well make it the day of her birthday. Ironic, to reunite estranged mother and daughter on her thirtieth birthday.

She pressed send, and her e-mail sped off to some immeasurably distant place.

Mother was head of PR at MegaHard E-Publishing Corp. She was legendary in contemporary cultural marketing. It sounds ironic, but the new high-tech publishing industry was heavily dependent on traditional direct marketing tactics. Momo's mother had started out years ago as a low-level saleswoman, struggling to make inroads into the then-tiny direct marketing world.

When demand for printed products crashed in the early twenty-first century, the e-publishing industry stepped in, swallowing up existing markets for printed materials and reinvigorating consumer interest in reading.

It was a huge cultural shift, and it also garnered support from all the national governments. After migration, there was a profound sense of the importance of cultural preservation. Laserdiscs made an ideal cultural repository: condense all of humanity's wisdom onto a disc and it would be preserved in perpetuity. Even the most rotten aspects of civilization could be saved onto a laserdisc without generating much stench. So the various governments universally supported the development of a discbook market.

And thus began the New Renaissance. The name sounds inspiring, but in practical terms it just meant that twenty-first-century writers could still make a living. Or at least not starve. You could make a reasonable comparison between the New Renaissance and the European Renaissance: MegaHard was its Medici. After a bitter rivalry, MegaHard's disc publishing operation had prevailed over Microsoft (the company behind that super successful late twentieth-century Windows operating system) to become the mainstay of the publishing industry. MegaHard touted its brand name as visionary, communicating gravitas, strength, and power, though all along some people found it distasteful: it sounded rapacious and overbearing.

Mother was one of the first discbook direct marketing salespeople whom MegaHard recruited. Her stellar track record initially earned her a role as a research assistant in the direct marketing division, but she rose through the ranks and before long was division head. The secret to Mother's meteoric rise was her inspiration to include a free "Panacea Virus Protection Kit" disc with every set of encyclopedias she sold. The disc included tutorials demonstrating how customers could remove the most commonly contracted computer viruses. It also included instructions on how to get rid of the many foodborne and airborne bacteria and viruses that proliferated in the twenty-first century. It even offered advice on how to do drugs without becoming addicted. The Panacea Virus Protection Kit was a huge hit with consumers, virtually guaranteeing Mother's promotion. Mother had gone all out to promote sales of the disc; she even modeled for the illustrated instructions. Her face was kind and persuasive, and left a deep impression on readers as they watched her demonstrate expunging a virus.

Momo was twenty-three when Mother was promoted to head of direct marketing, and had only just earned her license as a DMT (dermal maintenance technician). Momo hated the idea of using her relationship with her powerful mother to advance her career. She bit the bullet and worked hard, managing her career herself, and before long—despite being a newcomer to the profession—she won the Creative Cosmetics Prize for the Asia-Pacific region. For her prize-winning masterpiece, Momo transformed a lovely Indonesian girl into a mythic canary. She named the piece "The Unbearable Lightness of Being," and with her newfound fame and fortune she opened her own salon, the eponymous Salon Canary. Once Momo started getting attention, it came out that she was the "pride and joy" of the head of direct marketing for MegaHard.

"If you would be so kind as to play down the fact that I'm her 'pride and joy' . . . It suggests that I only got where I am professionally because of her. But I got here entirely on my own. I started from the ground up and I've never asked for special treatment. Please show some respect for my professional training."

At first she was reluctant to say more to the media. But one of her clients was a reporter and urged her to clarify herself in a statement. The reporter was Tomie Ito.

The media, however, saw an opportunity to fashion Momo into a kind of role model. Self-motivated, with real prospects and a pretty pedigree, she was too cool: a rebel star for a new age. But Momo wanted nothing to do with the distortions of fame. She wanted only to sequester herself in her new salon space. Yet while the e-magazine gossip embarrassed her, it guaranteed a steady stream of clients. Good thing Momo wasn't the pushy type and hated the limelight so much. Otherwise her jealous competition might have ganged up on her and dispatched a terrorist to blow up Salon Canary.

Was this not the successful career that Momo had envisioned?

Yet she felt like she'd never really enjoyed the fruits of her labor. Instead, she felt like she was always battling to get to some urgent destination that she couldn't even name.

Battling . . . In the most primitive sense, a battle is when a couple of insects or wild animals or humans go head to head to see who comes out on top.

But Momo's war was more complicated than that. The combat stretched out indefinitely. She couldn't stand that her opponent dismissed all her hard work, so even though Momo knew it was absurd to keep fighting, she held her ground. Momo wasn't trying to show off; she didn't stage this ongoing battle to intimidate her enemies. She battled to reinforce her self-worth. She believed that if she just stood her ground, she would surely win . . . or at the very least—given that her opponent had a wealth of resources and this was a war without weapons—she wouldn't be the loser.

If Momo gave up, on the other hand, then the combat would come to an end. Victory and defeat would mean nothing, and all her effort, all her persistence would have been in vain. A bubble rising to the surface of the ocean, bursting in the light of the sun.

It all sounded ridiculous when you said it out loud, even to Momo. Yet she felt she couldn't think of it in rational terms. This was personal.

Her adversary was her own mother, after all.

And she resented her.

Momo blamed her unhappy childhood on Mother. She left home for boarding school so she wouldn't have to deal with

Mother. It was so enraging: she expected sadness, for Mother to be kind to her, to try to reconcile with her, to plead tearfully with her to come home. But she did none of those things. Mother didn't even bother to ask about her daughter's trials in the Dermal Maintenance Academy!

And so let them fight. See who caved in first.

And yet . . . Momo still wondered pathetically to herself whether Mother only cared about MegaHard. Was there no room in her heart for her daughter?

Momo later figured that maybe her relationship with Mother was strictly biological. Wasn't the meaning imposed on family not destiny but all just socially constructed anyway? So she and Mother just happened to cross paths for a time in the world, who cares? Why make a big deal of it?

And yet each time she saw Mother's "businesswoman" smile on a discbook, her heart filled with an indescribable rage. *You hypocrite! You forget your own daughter even as you greet your customers with a grin!*

She told herself she would have a good life alone. *Just watch, Mother.*

Yet now her greatest competitor was coming to see her.

Momo and Andy sat on the floor, facing each other in silence. They were enclosed by yellow wallpaper and illuminated by beams of light cast down by the skylight. Girl and dog needed no words. The little dog Andy was calm and clean and tidy, nearly as easy to care for as a robot dog. Momo cut a slice of peach and fed it to him.

She found it odd: she'd always refused to have housemates, yet here she was, taking care of a dog! And she hadn't gotten the dog out of loneliness. At thirty, Momo interacted with all kinds of clients, though she limited herself to professional conversations. She didn't want to get close to anyone. She preferred to live quietly on her own. When she first graduated from the Dermal Maintenance Academy ten years earlier, she was new to the field and had no choice but to start out in a huge general practice. That salon was affiliated with Microsoft (Momo didn't want her boss to be connected to MegaHard too). All the young clinicians took walk-in clients in treatment rooms as tiny as pigeon cages. Momo couldn't stand practicing the art of dermal maintenance in such a sterile space.

She had no say in the length or location of the consultation: the company strictly regulated each dermal maintenance session. She couldn't select which clients to treat; too often she was forced to take clients who were uncooperative or with whom she couldn't communicate. When she thought about being just one among many new clinicians working on a floor full of pigeon cages, she felt like one of those metallic factory droids laboring on the surface of the earth, without an ounce of creativity! And she hated the daily grind of starting and finishing a shift. It made her feel like a cog in the machine. But Momo was no cog. She'd already endured the group mentality of boarding school and had no desire to do it again!

It was a struggle, but by twenty-three, Momo's hard work paid off and she became a certified dermal care technician. Then she won the Creative Cosmetics Prize for the Asia-Pacific region. And at last she had enough money to leave the general practice behind and establish her own clinic: Salon Canary.

So for two decades—from age ten to twenty when she attended boarding school, and from twenty to thirty when she worked as a professional dermal maintenance technician—Momo was forced to be close to people. Often quite literally: dermal care meant you didn't just look at people's faces. You had to see, touch, penetrate their bodies. Naked bodies. This kind of physical intimacy might have been a turn-on for someone else—Momo's former classmates, even perhaps her clients—but Momo disliked it.

The year that Momo's breasts began to grow and black pubic hairs began to sprout, a passion for Momo swelled up in a female classmate she was often paired with for practicums. Pairs of students took turns massaging each other's naked bodies and applying various kinds of lotion. This poor girl was paired with Momo. Lola was a white girl who had just emigrated from New America to the Asia-Pacific district. She had the pale, delicate features of a vintage Barbie Doll. Lola caressed Momo's body and before long felt like offering her heart up to Momo to massage in return: she fell hard for her. The girl tried to approach Momo, but Momo didn't notice. Suspiciously, she asked Momo: "Aren't you yourself a girl? You don't like girls? You mean you like boys?!" This just enraged Momo, who felt humiliated and ignored the girl even more. Momo felt that, as a dermal care technician, you should keep your professional intimacies and your personal intimacies entirely separate. But the girl couldn't take it, and in the middle of the night she burst into Momo's dorm room, totally naked, and wrapped herself up in the white sheets of Momo's bed. She begged Momo to hold her. But Momo just sat there at her desk reading discbooks, slowly and deliberately doing her nails. Momo felt her body was private property. For Momo, treating her clients' skin was no different from a stockbroker helping clients make trades. But when it came to her body, she had no interest in getting involved and no interest in joining her clients. She managed it alone.

The girl ran from Momo's room in tears that night.

"Momo, you've touched me in our practice sessions. Why are you ignoring me now?"

Momo had grabbed the nail clippers and jabbed at the girl's pale white throat with a crescent stroke, piercing the skin. Blood gushed out. Momo hadn't meant to hurt the girl, just to scare her off, and maybe test her own skills: she knew she could repair any scars on Lola's neck in class and restore the skin to smooth perfection. But Momo would never get the chance to show her skill: though she felt strongly that public and private intimacies should be totally separate, what she failed to grasp was that private conflicts could easily spill over into public spheres. The girl's heart was broken. She refused to partner with Momo in class ever again.

This kind of thing continued to happen to Momo, but she reacted less violently; she could understand people being attracted to her. Perhaps her characteristic aloofness, combined with her beauty, paradoxically drove her admirers more crazy. But the distance she cultivated was genuinely unbridgeable. You could look from a safe distance but never touch.

Momo knew that Tomie Ito, who had been making advances toward her for a long time and taking opportunities to get close, was one such admirer.

It made Momo's decision to join the dermal maintenance profession feel like a big mistake. Why was her heart set on this job?

She could just as easily have chosen a more solitary profession, like a novelist. Why did she have to choose a job reliant on intimacy?

When Momo made up her mind to become a dermal care technician, it was entirely her own idea, and she stuck with it stubbornly for twenty years.

In 2080, when she was ten, Momo left home and her mother to attend a distant boarding school and learn a challenging craft. She graduated at twenty and had been working ever since. The reasons for her dogged determination were complex, and even at thirty she didn't fully understand them. Sometimes she even suspected that the life she now had as an adult wasn't the product of personal effort but rather the result of a formless snarl of nameless hands pushing her to where she now stood. Maybe she was like a chess piece. Or a tiny screw in a factory on the surface somewhere, being installed deep in the body of an M unit by the fireproof hands of a cyborg. . . .

Why was she so stubborn? Why did she always make harsh decisions and then stick to them even when they weren't necessarily good for her? Momo knew the answer all too well: her obstinacy preserved her autonomy. In her short life, too many important decisions had already been made for her by someone else. Even irrational decisions. She'd rather make a poor decision for herself, acting on her own desires, than have it made by someone else.

She didn't want to be some screw in a factory ever again. It felt like being a patient admitted to the hospital and anaesthetized only to learn that she'd undergone major surgery and that all of her vital organs had been shuffled around beyond recognition while she was asleep!

Momo had read in a disczine about the organ trade at the end of the twentieth century. It had grown to the point where many a wealthy but sick Arab tourist would bribe a doctor into surreptitiously anaesthetizing some hapless patient from the Indian hinterlands—who'd been tricked into coming in to the hospital for a "free check-up"—and scooping out one of the poorer fellow's kidneys, only to transplant it into the rich person's body in the adjoining room. Upon awakening from his anaesthetic dreams, the Indian patient would leave the hospital and notice a peculiar scar. But it wouldn't be until he was next admitted to the hospital that he would learn that his own organ, his kidney, was gone!

In the end, who had the right to decide what happened to a person's body? To their life?

Momo shivered at the thought.

Perhaps the resonance of this profound question for Momo explained her uneasy reaction regarding treatment for her troublesome finger.

Once again she had taken advice from an outsider and obediently relinquished her body to the care of others! Did her body belong to her or did it belong to someone else? Or did her body belong to her craft, dermal care? If her body was indeed her own, then wasn't it up to her whether she kept the finger or used it until it rotted off? It was her finger, it was nobody' else's business. . . . In the end, for the sake of her job, she had no choice: she went ahead and dutifully had it replaced. In thirty years, it was the sole exception she made.

Just because Momo resisted intimacy with others, that didn't mean she was self-obsessed.

Momo believed the human body contained a kind of hormone-releasing gland or organ. This hormone could stimulate intimate connections between people, so that people with a high concentration enjoyed social intercourse, while people with a lower concentration were more reclusive. Momo, like the twentieth-century Indian patient, felt she'd been placed on the operating table and had her hormone-producing gland plucked out at some point without her knowing it. Probably well before puberty.

The scar from this gland's removal still felt sensitive to Momo, and troubled her in a way she found hard to face. It felt bitterly ironic to think that her functional, vital gland was now nothing but a faint mark.

Momo's most important organ had been taken from her when she was still so very little.

Obstinate Momo, who insisted on living alone, nonetheless agreed to take Andy from Tomie Ito. She disliked accepting other people's decisions on principle and had no desire for a roommate—even a dog. Was this an exception?

This time Momo knew she wasn't just making an exception. Perhaps it was just the dog's name: Andy.

It didn't matter to Momo whether or not Andy was a factory-produced robot dog. Andy was a real dog and therefore rare and valuable—but Momo didn't love him any more or less. It annoyed her to deal with a real dog's food, water, piss, and shit, but wasn't a big deal to her. Plus Andy was uncommonly well behaved. He liked to lick people, but apart from that he wasn't dirty, and he didn't bark or fuss much when clients came over; he just stood to the side wagging his tail quietly and staring at them with his wide eyes. Momo rarely went out, and Andy had never ventured outside—so perhaps he had no desire to leave the house. He'd come to Momo when he was still a puppy, so maybe he didn't even realize that there was a whole world beyond this house.

Like the mythical canary?

With all four paws on the ground, Andy drew his body back like a bow with his front paws planted and his butt in the air. He opened his mouth wide and gave a big yawn, rice-colored fur bristling as he stretched. He looked content.

When they were alone, Momo would talk to Andy, stroking the fine close fur outlining his pink gums and shiny white teeth. Andy couldn't reply, and wouldn't bark. But he would lick the pores on the back of Momo's hand with his purpley-red tongue.

But in Momo's heart there lived another Andy, both quieter and more restless than this one—

Momo understood that this other Andy existed only inside of her. As if she were pregnant. But Momo's relationship to this Andy was not that of mother and daughter. They were sisters.

Momo was convinced that it was her inside Andy who was responsible for those montagelike dreams she had, full of the chrome-colored remnants of the mechanical civilization on the surface.

Once she dreamed that M units were battling in the street. She could hear the raw static from the android factory and see the desolate solar fields extending far into the distance.

She dreamed she was lying in the middle of the broiling Asian desert, ultraviolet rays infusing her chestnut-black hair until it turned to brittle limestone and broke off as she lay there, utterly alone—

Momo had lived alone as long as she could remember—she was used to it. If not for her job, she might as well be living with only a computer for company on some radioactive desert island. But she didn't mind having Andy in her life and was always whispering sweet nothings to him.

Andy reminded her of her very earliest memories from long, long ago, counting backward from thirty, when her sweet life ended and her solitary career began.

From when she was living in the children's ward of the hospital deep beneath the sea.

From some extremely ordinary decade near the end of the twenty-first century.

# 5

As a child, Momo was in very fragile health.

In 2077, at age seven, she was admitted to the hospital.

The doctors discovered she was suffering from a number of bizarre pathologies, including the mysterious LOGO virus. Only a series of complex, specialized operations could cure all her various ailments.

While the clinicians prepared for the procedures, she had to live in a fully sterile hospital room. They said it was to protect her, to prevent her from catching more infections while she was so weak. But she felt like a lonely bird, abandoned in the prison of a tiny cage. She was an impatient child to begin with, so in Momo's memory of events she was stranded interminably in a borderless gray space with no one to save her. Adults came and went, administering tests and sometimes giving her anaesthetics so they could experiment with minor surgeries. They claimed that it was all for Momo's own good.

During her endless stay in the hospital, she didn't even see much of her mother. Momo's condition was rare, and her treatment extremely expensive. The subsidies from National Health Insurance were just a drop in the bucket. At the time, her mother was still just a low-level marketer for MegaHard. She had to get extra work and take out loans. She could only video conference with Momo every now and then when she had a spare moment. Mostly, all she saw on the screen was Momo's pouting face peeking out from her lonely hospital bed.

That was more or less when Momo started to hate video conference calls.

By then, video conference calls had completely replaced voice calling to streamline effective communication. But even back then little Momo could see how ridiculous this "effective communication" really was. People can't get close enough to hug, so they invent a "communication" device that can replace hugging. How absurd!

Mother hadn't hugged her in a long time. And the Doctor Aunties and the Uncle Nurses didn't hug her. Everyone said it was because they were afraid of passing germs from outside on to Momo. Her solitary life in the hospital was her first experience of being alone, and looking back, she could hardly imagine a more drawn-out, excruciating weaning period.

The ironic thing was, the hospital staff were aware of how lonely Momo was. It's just that their attention was focused on more practical matters.

The clinicians worried that Momo would have trouble reintegrating into society if she didn't make friends with healthy children her own age. So they brought Momo a very clean playmate.

One dark afternoon, woozy from the effects of anaesthesia and wiped out from repeated blood draws for check-ups, Momo saw through her dreamlike medicated haze the best friend she would ever have in her life: Andy.

Doctor Auntie said: "This is Andy. Andy has been fully sterilized and disinfected, so she is one hundred times cleaner than the doctors, nurses, and Mother, and so will make a perfect friend for you." Andy was the same size as Momo, and like Momo she had peach-colored cheeks. But she was much sweeter and better-behaved than Momo. She never pouted the way Momo did.

When Momo first saw a young girl materialize in the hospital ward, she couldn't help feeling suspicious, and she resisted. Momo knew that adults loved to play tricks on kids. This adorable child was probably just another trick! Like when Mother tricked her into coming to the hospital in the first place.

But lonely little Momo eventually relented. She had no choice. Besides, her new playmate was pretty adorable, and as the hospital had hoped, they became friends. Momo accepted Andy into every part of her life, and the two children did everything together, 24/7, eating, sleeping, bathing.

Momo had watched discbook primers about psychoanalysis. The discbooks mentioned the twentieth-century French psychoanalyst Jacques Lacan, and quoted Lacan as saying that very young children cannot distinguish the difference between self and other. Only between six and eighteen months of age, when a child looks in a mirror (including symbolic as well as material mirrors), will she acquire an individual sense of self. By looking in the mirror, the toddler realizes that in the mirror world there is a child just like herself, whose every move is the exact mirror of her own, and yet who is not her. A child's awareness of her own existence depends on the existence of this "other," and this window between six and eighteen months is so significant it's known as the "Mirror Stage."

Looking back, Momo felt that her time together with Andy in the hospital was her second Mirror Stage: Andy resembled her but was not her. And she only realized how lonely she'd been when Andy appeared.

She realized she couldn't always keep herself company. She needed someone else.

Sometimes the doctors and Mother would watch her and Andy playing house and other games on a monitor screen. Momo really hated people monitoring her from outside the ward. She disliked these sneaky grown-ups. Besides Mother, only one of them was attractive: a trim, pretty, South Asian-looking woman who sometimes appeared among them.

Once Mother called Momo from a business trip:

"Momo? Are you having fun with Andy?"

"Mother! Why doesn't Andy have a pee-pee, but I do?"

"Momo . . . after your surgery, you'll be just like Andy."

"Can I lend my pee-pee to Andy to play with?"

"No more playing doctor! Why don't you read a few more of the discbooks that Mother brought you?"

Mother had recently installed a custom multimedia discbook computer in Momo's room.

Besides playing doctor (grown-up Momo didn't know why she loved playing doctor so much as a child when she hated doctors and clinics so much as an adult), Momo and Andy also discussed more serious topics, such as the children's discbook version of *Hamlet* that MegaHard had published.

In the discbook, Hamlet said: "I could be bounded in a nutshell and count myself a king of infinite space, were it not that I have bad dreams."

This made sense to the two girls, except they thought "king" should be changed to "princesses." They vowed that when they got out of the hospital, they would get married and live happily ever after. They'd also have two little princess children.

Mother called again and said she'd noticed Momo and Andy talking and laughing. What were they talking about?

"None of your business."

This was Momo's stock answer in the ward.

"Momo . . ."

"It's a secret. It's none of your business."

"Momo, your surgery is coming up. Are you nervous?"

"None. Of. Your. Business!"

While they were quarantined in the ward together, Momo could hug and kiss Andy without fear of catching anything, because Andy had been completely decontaminated using a high-heat disinfection process. For the first time Momo felt an emotion stronger than "need." Before, she felt "need" for Mother, but now that Andy was in her life, Momo longed only for her.

So much so that Momo even wished she could get inside Andy's body, and have Andy get inside of hers. . . . She didn't quite understand what "sex" was yet, but she fantasized about "eating": she wanted to eat Andy up until she was in her belly, and she wanted Andy to eat her up too. Little Momo thought that if they ate each other up, even just a bite of flesh, then she and Andy would really become one person, and Andy would never leave her like Mother.

So Momo told Andy: "I want to eat a bite of your flesh." And Andy didn't refuse. Instead she spread her fingers in front of Momo's face. Momo wasn't greedy—she bit down on just one finger, the middle one of Andy's right hand, though she worried it would hurt her. But Andy's face stayed totally serene. With great difficulty Momo bit off Andy's entire middle finger. No blood came out. She chewed it patiently but it was really hard to break down, and she spit it out. She was happy to forget it—her teeth were hurting. She also wanted Andy to take a bite of her, but was reluctant to part with a finger. So Momo lifted up her skirt and told Andy to eat her little pee-pee. She didn't like it anyway. It was just an annoying bit of flesh. Andy didn't have that organ, and besides, it was going to be removed in the surgery anyway. No harm in giving it to Andy now.

Except it hurt!!!

When Andy bit down, before she even broke the skin, Momo was rolling on the floor in agony. Apparently she couldn't just randomly have someone bite off a part of her body that she didn't like . . .

That's when she and Andy stopped playing doctor.

Even though they stopped, the adults still found out. A doctor saw on a monitor that Andy was missing her middle finger, and asked what happened. Surprisingly, she didn't seem particularly upset with Momo and didn't scold her. Doctor Auntie just reminded her:

"Play all you want. After your surgery, you'll regret not playing more. But please don't eat each other—otherwise we'll have nothing left to work with." She added: "Momo, eating Andy's finger will come back to haunt you later."

Momo didn't understand what she meant.

She heard so many things as a child that she only understood once she grew up.

She felt this even more keenly having her finger transplant at age thirty.


But little Momo's surgery was over before she knew it.

On the day of the surgery, Uncle Nurse had anaesthetized her as usual, and she fell into a deep sleep. She thought she was just having another minor procedure. She never imagined that this would be the final, great rite of passage: like preparing a soldier for battle, this megaoperation required thirteen doctors performing simultaneous surgeries. Momo's body was the Last Supper, laid out like a carcass on the operating table. Although she couldn't witness the massacre that was her body in that moment, she could see something nobody else could.

Momo saw two bright white figures floating in the gloom between heaven and earth. It was her and her, Momo and Andy. They wandered in a city crisscrossed by canals. Where was this city? Momo vaguely recalled reading about a place like this in the Shakespeare discbook on *Merchant of Venice*. . . . The two figures broke through the dense fog. They wore gold and silver masks painted with tears, like the Joker in a deck of cards. They held hands, they danced, but when they tried to kiss, the masks prevented their lips touching. Andy began to lift Momo's body up and up until she was sitting on Andy's head.

Then Andy pressed Momo's body against her skull so hard that she was injected into Andy's skull like a needle into a vein. Once inside Andy's skull, Momo could hear Andy whisper softly:

*You are a canary in a cage.*

Then Momo woke up.

Mother sat beside her. She was no longer in the hermetically sealed-off hospital ward. She could see an open window. Through the window she saw a tree, and from the tree hung a single dead leaf, fluttering in the breeze. Yes, the window was definitely open—a cool draft blew over Momo's prone body. It wasn't air conditioning.

There was no sign of Andy.

"Momo, the surgery was a success!" Mother said, elated. "You don't have to stay in a sterile hospital room anymore. Now you can stay in a normal ward with a window and watch the leaves."

"Mother, where is Andy?"

"And I have more good news for you: Mother has been promoted. I'm not just a run-of-the-mill sales representative anymore. I'm now a marketing director. From now on we're going to be much better off."

"Where's Andy?"

Mother didn't reply. She just shared those two pieces of good news. But Momo felt ambivalent: yes, the surgery was successful, so Momo could leave the hospital—but where was Andy? And yes, Mother had been promoted—but wouldn't that just mean Momo would see her even less than she did now?

Momo asked one last question before they left the hospital.

"Mother, what is a 'canary'?"

" 'Canary'? My darling Momo, we can look it up in the discbook animal encyclopedia when we get home, okay?"

Then Mother told her she loved her dearly.

The year was 2080. Momo was ten. She'd lived in the hospital for three years.


It was only years later, as a young woman at boarding school studying hard to be a dermal care technician, that Momo finally stumbled upon some information about "canaries."

As a teenager she'd almost forgotten the term, but once when she was looking up the entry for "gold leaf" in the encyclopedia, she glimpsed the words "gilded sparrow" in the term's etymology and recalled that someone had mentioned a word like that to her once. "Gold leaf facials" were super trendy in the Asia-Pacific region when Momo was in school—they involved applying a thin coat of gold leaf to the client's face, as the name suggests. Though the technique may have been inspired by the famous King Tutankhamun and his golden mask, it wasn't Egypt where this technique was most popular. Rather it was in New Taiwan, where the gold-digging

Taiwanese took the old expression about "gilding your face in gold (to make yourself look good)" quite literally. But Momo didn't get it, so she looked it up in the encyclopedia discbook.

In the entry on canaries, a news item from old Japan caught her eye—it was dated spring 1995.

According to the discbook, on an ordinary morning that spring someone had released poison gas in a Tokyo subway, injuring and even killing many innocent passengers. The Japanese government named the Aum Shinrikyo cult as the prime suspect. When the police raided the cult's headquarters, they found the chemical ingredients required to make toxic gas. Heavily armed and wearing gas masks, the police force alarmed people so much they thought some kind of major disaster had occurred. A huge manhunt was under way, and nobody dared joke about it. Perhaps the only point of levity was the fact that, in addition to being armed to the teeth, the police also carried cages with canaries inside.

Yes, canaries. Wasn't it a silly image, to imagine the armed policemen, formal and proper, carrying caged canaries up the mountain? Though not for the canaries—for them it was an unparalleled tragedy. These beautiful, delicate little birds, with no chance to fly or sing, just accompanying the police to battle. Because the police were fully outfitted with gasproof gear, they had no way of sensing the colorless, odorless gas, or of knowing where it was emanating from—this was beyond the capacity of the human nose! So humans employed sacrificial canaries. Let the sarin gas take the lives of canaries instead of our invincible human defenders.

And so the police used the canaries as bait. If a bird showed signs of shock or died suddenly, it signaled that the toxin was in the vicinity of the cage. Without them, the police wouldn't find the poison gas. Canaries died so humans could live.

Momo had no idea how many canaries the police used in their raids that day. The encyclopedia didn't include that information; it wasn't considered valuable enough.

Among the green hills
a troop of soldiers in black leave a gray factory
petals of cadmium yellow scatter among the green grass
each one a murdered canary
sarin gas the birds' lament.

Even so, humans locked them in cages to keep them from flying away. They were caged not because humanity cherished them, but to torture them.

Why then, Momo wondered, did Andy call me a canary?

Momo now recalled encountering the word "canary" in a twentieth-century Argentinian novel called *Kiss of the Spider Woman*. The book mentioned a "panther woman," half human and half beast, who could transform into a panther. When she was in a human state, she played happily with her caged canaries, but as soon as she began to transform into a panther, the canaries could smell it on her breath and would die on the spot. Typically, readers sympathized with the panther woman. But not Momo. She felt for the forgotten little birds. The panther could at least enjoy the passing thrill of biting into a bloody snack; at least her claws and teeth were put to their intended use, her talents weren't wasted. Canaries lived their entire lives with wings and yet could never leave their tiny metal cages, let alone fly! The outside world was filled with terror and beauty, but they would never know either. They were trapped like trinkets in a toy chest, forever at the mercy of others.

Momo recalled that she and Andy had read Shakespeare's *The Tempest* together in the hospital. In act 5, scene 1, after having lived on a desert island for many years, Miranda delivers her famous speech in which she reveals her vision of this mortal world: "O wonder!/ How many goodly creatures are there here!/ How beauteous mankind is! O brave new world/ That has such people in it!"

By the end of the play, like a canary flying free from its cage, Miranda returns to live in the beautiful world just as she's always dreamed. But there was nothing in the play about what happened to her afterward. Did Miranda regret going back to her father's land? Did she escape the panthers and poison gas of the world beyond her cage? Having flown free, how did she know the outside world wasn't just another, slightly bigger cage?

Perhaps it was Momo's ambivalence that kept the well-known dermal care technician single and living a simple life at age thirty. Living and working out of Salon Canary, she was indifferent to the fact that people might associate the name with the beautiful isolation of a vintage birdcage. She was a celebrity in T City, but Momo had never been involved in a sex scandal. There were no rumors of her having a girlfriend or boyfriend. She didn't subscribe to any pornographic disczines like *Playgirl, Playboy, Sappho,* or *Dyke.* Momo just lived alone, pure and simple. She didn't seem to worry about feeling lonely and seemed to have no sexual needs. She had no intention of practicing Buddhism and didn't subscribe to any religion.

Momo claimed to be used to this life.

Few celebrity dermal care technicians in T City were as reclusive as Momo. Few of them earned their lofty socioeconomic status by cultivating the quiet life.

The dermal care trade had become one of the most respected professions of the twenty-first century.

Though the bulk of humanity had retreated to the ocean floor to avoid lethal radiation, the nightmarish psychological scars remained. Ultraviolet skin-damage prevention practices had become second nature. Not only that, but living deep beneath the ocean in an entirely artificial environment had weakened the skin's natural protective qualities, so it now required even more maintenance. And an unfortunate but common side effect of the compulsory AIDS vaccine was allergic skin reactions. As a result, young, old, male, female . . . everyone in the twenty-first-century Asia Pacific was preoccupied with skin care. What's more, dermal care had evolved so quickly that it now played a major role in driving both consumer need and consumer desire. The twentieth century's obsession with fashion had all been funneled into the world of the dermal care industry.

The twentieth-century Spanish director Almodovar had flaunted the latest in European fashion in movies like *High Heels* and *Kika*. Robert Altman's *Prêt-à-Porter* went further, draping to the point of obscuring an array of the hottest movie stars head to toe in the so-called experimental fashion by the great designers. But that was ancient history now—it didn't fit the time anymore. In the first part of *Prêt-à-Porter*, Altman remarks that the film isn't about the naked body but is rather an investigation of how fashion is used to *conceal* the body. Yet the movie is so congested with clothing that it barely shows any skin! Vintage fashion movies of the old world prioritized the flesh. *The Soft Skin* (known in Chinese by the hackneyed title *Soft Jade and Warm Fragrance*) by the French director Truffaut is a great example of this. *The Soft Skin* doesn't appeal to contemporary tastes; only twentieth-century humans would emphasize sensuality over skin quality. Big names in the fashion world like Chanel, Calvin Klein, Versace, and Armani had long ago followed the example of brands like Lancome, Christian Dior, and Shiseido and shifted

their focus to beauty products. Once the AIDS vaccine elimi-
nated anxiety around sex, having a thriving, diverse sex life not
only was openly accepted, it became humanity's principal leisure
activity. Nowadays sexual etiquette called for gleaming, soft skin
in bed—not for lingerie emblazoned with some gaudy label.
Truth be told, a young girl in the new world who had never had
skin care treatments would look more like a wrinkly old elephant
than an old lady who'd practiced skin care religiously [Note:
MegaHard's animal encyclopedia defines "elephant" as a terres-
trial mammal that existed before the twenty-first century—and
people generally don't enjoy picturing extinct animals when they
are making love.]

Consequently a highly regarded dermal care technician
enjoyed a higher status than twentieth-century designers like Rei
Kawakubo and Issey Miyake. They earned enough to live the
conspicuous life of a socialite, throwing never-ending banquets,
tables laid with so much meat, money, and power that even a
king of gourmands could never eat it all. This was the culture
now. These were the instigators of the "3B" movement in T City:
Body, Books, Beauty. A great body paired with refined reading
habits was the height of beauty.

So it was rare to find a dermal care technician as reclusive as
Momo.

She hardly went out at all. For contact with the outside world
she depended largely on two machines. One was her personal
worldlink multi-media computer, and the other was her scanner. The computer offered her seamless access to information,
while the scanner met the needs of her senses.

Besides using the computer to access the latest news from
the aesthetics industry, she also used it to manage her clients.
She could keep track of client bookings, prepare her daily
schedule, and record each client's individual skincare needs.

Liver spots? Pockmarks? Ringworm? Did the skin tend to the acid or the base? How well did it resist air pollution and ultraviolet radiation? Allergic reactions to the AIDS vaccine? How did it respond to alpha-hydroxy solutions for keratin removal? Momo kept track of these and any other minor changes her clients' bodies experienced.

Momo was detail-oriented and professional. She didn't employ anyone to help with data entry; she did it herself. Each client had a case file, and each file had a place in her hard drive, just as the stars each had their place in the heavens. She kept a record of results each time a client used M skin so that she wouldn't miss even the tiniest detail. She took pleasure in recording even the most mundane aspects of her clients' copious medical histories. And in keeping such detailed records, naturally Momo also took every precaution, establishing firewalls to protect her data from viruses and multiple layers of password protection to ward off prying eyes. If other members of her profession ever got hold of this classified information, they'd be seriously impressed; if her clients saw it, they'd be shocked. If a client ever did break into her database, she'd probably never work again; no one would trust her.

Even in this most decadent age, willful moral transgression still terrified most people.

When Momo was ten she played with a toy "scanner." Once the scanner connected wirelessly to her computer, it could scan remote images and transmit them to the computer, allowing her to see the data it had gathered on the screen.

In fact, a variety of scanners existed—they didn't necessarily come with lenses, radar, or cables. There were even scanners made from emulsions that the average person wouldn't know how to use. The insatiable curiosity of humankind had produced an abundance of scanners.

At thirty Momo still played with scanners, but of course they were different from the computer games she'd had at ten. The latest generation of scanner produced far more complex and realistic multidimensional images, and you couldn't buy one at a regular computer or electronics store.

Not long after Momo had opened her private salon, a familiar Indian woman named Draupadi showed up at her door. Momo hadn't seen her in many years, but she'd never forgotten her.

"What an exceptional name you've chosen, 'Salon Canary.' I'm sure your technique is just as lovely," commented the woman. "I'm curious—who does 'canary' refer to? What does it mean?"

Draupadi was the one who brought Momo the new scanner, to congratulate her on her new salon.

Draupadi couldn't have bought this latest generation of scanner on the open market—maybe it was even contraband. It was unbelievably cool. Not only did the scanner benefit Momo's business by allowing her deeper insights into her clients' bodies, it plunged her into a deep sea of delights: there was no line between "understanding" her clients' bodies and "sneaking a peek" at them. From the privacy of her tiny room she could access the countless intimate experiences of a myriad of people.

Now Momo had even less reason to fear being alone.

This scanner was actually critical in the use of M skin. M skin's chief purpose was not to maintain the skin, but to carry out a far more unusual mission.

M skin was applied lotionlike to the entire surface of a person's body. It could sense and then classify everything the body felt: pain, itches, temperature, arousal, sexual contact. Had the skin come in contact with another body? What sex were they?

Was the skin touching plastic or metal? The M skin tracked and digitized it all.

You see, "M skin" was short for "memory skin": skin with a memory function. After it had been removed, all the data it had gathered could be entered into the scanner and interpreted.

Take the M skin she had just removed from Tomie Ito, for example. She came to Salon Canary every seven days to replace her M skin, which recorded a week of skin memories. These might be anything from scratches or mosquito bites to work, sex, meals, and discharge of fluids. The data recorded by M skin varied substantially depending on the part of the body involved: the stimuli to the fingertips produced vastly more data than, say, the buttocks, since fingers were more often left exposed by clothing. Yet Momo's computer and scanner processed all this complex and diverse information fastidiously. Once it was all entered into the computer, that stimulus of every moment (captured at ten-second intervals) would appear onscreen.

In the simplified chart below, the symbols $, #, and @ each represent a different stimulus (of course in reality there were many more than just three); the number of occurrences of each symbol represents the intensity of stimuli for that interval.

A chart like the following shows just seven of the total 6,048,800 seconds in seven days of Tomie Ito's life, or 1/8,640 of total available data. And this seven seconds of data was restricted to Tomie's left ventral groin, a tiny fraction of all the skin on the body! This area of skin had received multiple forms of stimulation, but Momo focused on just a few factors ($, #, and @ all being associated with sexual arousal).

You can extrapolate the sheer magnitude of data harvested by M skin. Luckily Momo's computer had the power to crunch all the mysteries of the universe down into manageable data that could then be recorded onto a laserdisc, the only thing with the

## Specimen: Tomie Ito No. B069/
## Location: Left ventral groin

### 樣本: 伊藤富江　NO:B069/部位: 左鼠蹊部

| 9 |  |  |  | $ | $ |  |  |
|---|---|---|---|---|---|---|---|
| 8 |  |  |  | $@ | $ |  | @ |
| 7 |  |  | # | $#@ | $ | @ | @ |
| 6 | $ | $ | # | $#@ | $ | $@ | @ |
| 5 | $# | $ | $# | $#@ | $ | $#@ | @ |
| 4 | $#@ | $ | $#@ | $#@ | $# | $#@ | #@ |
| 3 | $#@ | $# | $#@ | $#@ | $# | $#@ | $#@ |
| 2 | $#@ | $#@ | $#@ | $#@ | $#@ | $#@ | $#@ |
| 1 | $#@ | $#@ | $#@ | $#@ | $#@ | $#@ | $#@ |
| 0 | 0:01:00 | 0:01:10 | 0:01:20 | 0:01:30 | 0:01:40 | 0:01:50 | 0:02:00 |

時間: 2100年2月8日午夜0時

**Time: 8 2400H FEB 2100**

capacity to store so much. You could say that the M skin discs Momo filed so meticulously in her salon were the most faithful record of her clients' sensual lives.

Naturally she had no intention of alerting her clients to M skin's memory function. They would never understand how critical this data was in Momo's profession; it would only frighten them, as if Momo had secretly read their private diaries. Instead Momo simply told them that M skin was a superior treatment that wasn't available at other salons. None of her clients had cause for suspicion. Every celebrity dermal care technician had their own special tricks of the trade that neither clients nor fellow professionals would ever know.

Never. How could all the debutantes and pretty boys who came to Salon Canary ever guess that Momo could use a dermal care product to peer into their bodies and know all their secrets?

From their M skin readouts, Momo could tell who had been constipated and when; who'd had gay sex and who'd had straight sex; who liked to get whipped during sex and then have a bottle of Kirin; which Don Juans and Medusas actually spent most of their time masturbating alone in their room. . . .

They would never fully understand. And neither could Momo. Why would Draupadi give her this dazzling gift with godlike powers? Perhaps Draupadi wanted to pass it along to the next generation? Draupadi had been a dermal care technician in another life; did she see that Momo stood out among her peers, and so gave her such an indispensable gift? Momo couldn't be sure.

She only knew that Draupadi had been a big influence on her decision to start in this line of work—in every sense, Draupadi was like a second mother to her. And Draupadi had taught her to read another kind of discbook—the secret diary of the body.

Because when all was said and done, reading the body through computer, scanner, and laserdisc was convoluted and indirect. In the end, the tables and code that flashed across her computer screen were no match for the power of firsthand, flesh-and-blood sensory reading. The best way to read the diary of the body was not through processing visual information, but by using the body—your own.

Draupadi taught Momo the most effective way to read M skin: once the data had been downloaded, it could be exported to Momo's own body.

All she had to do was paint herself with M skin, and the scanner would transmit her client's code onto Momo's fresh coat of M skin. Momo could then experience her client's sensations from the week as if they were her own.

Put simply, imagine the body is an old-style tape recorder and M skin is a cassette: every stimulus experienced by Tomie Ito's body was recorded like a sound. When Momo got the cassette and made a copy, she could play it in the tape recorder of her own body. And when playing it back, she experienced the pulse of sounds beating in her own body like the violent cacophony of a symphony without notes.

With this playback function, Momo knew everything that happened to the bodies of Tomie Ito and her other clients. With her M skin synced to the computer, she could experience:

Last weekend. Midnight. Tomie with a young woman and young man. Hurtling past the protective atmospheric membrane and swimming naked in the sea above . . . the three of them swimming past the Mariana Trench to the coral reefs of the South China Sea and embracing amid a school of fish . . . then transforming into bubbles . . .

Oh, what a lovely sensation—

Momo sighed. Everything. She felt the ecstasy of the encounter in every pore of her body.

She didn't need to leave the house for faraway places. Her clients expanded the scope of her senses. As long as her clients traveled to the ends of the earth, Momo could go there with them.

Far away. So close.

Maybe Momo didn't detest physical intimacy after all. Maybe she just didn't like the emotional entanglements that came along with physical relationships.

She feared that this kind of relationship would be exhausting, disappointing, and leave her feeling disillusioned. Any love worth cherishing could be cut short. She knew the anguish of grieving all too well. She couldn't risk it again—she'd suffered enough.

# 6

omo had always felt a complex tangle of emotions
about Mother.

She needed Mother, but not in a tender way: just
the vision of her mother's beautiful face imprinted like a code
on her memory gave her the courage to keep on living.

Where did these feelings come from?

They probably started when she was a child in the hospital.

Back then, Momo needed Mother in a pure way: all she
wanted were the cuddles that Mother routinely said she couldn't
provide because she was working overtime to pay Momo's hospital bills. But Momo sometimes felt sacrificed for Mother's
career. Sometimes she caught Mother looking at her on the monitor in the observation room. The first few times she caught her
looking, she felt pleased; but the longer she was in the hospital,
the more she thought Mother was laughing at her from outside
the ward. Why would you abandon your child and allow her no
human contact in the name of preventing contamination? With
no one to keep her company, all she could do to pass the time
was read the disczines that Mother sold for a living.

Momo looked up the statistics in the discbook encyclopedia for "Average Time Spent in a Pediatric Ward in

Twenty-First-Century Taiwan (single incident)" and saw that the figure was many times smaller than her own. She felt like she'd been set up. In the encyclopedia she read that children could sometimes be victims of "Unjust Imprisonment."

Good thing she had Andy to keep her company. Though she sensed that the adults were jealous of her relationship with Andy. Especially Mother.

Momo remembered Mother once asked her during a video call, "Momo, why have you been so quiet with Mother lately? Don't you like telling me stories anymore? Are you bored with the discbooks I brought you?"

"I don't read kids' stories anymore. They're too childish. Andy and I are reading Shakespeare."

"Did you understand *Romeo and Juliet*?"

"None. Of. Your. Business."

"Momo . . ."

"Forget it. I'm going to go read with Andy."

"Momo! Why do you only pay attention to Andy? You're ignoring me!"

It was obvious that Mother resented Momo's close relationship with Andy.

She was jealous.


Which was why, once the surgery was over and Momo discovered that Andy was missing, she immediately suspected it was Mother's doing.

Even though Mother later tried to explain that Andy wasn't really missing, that she was still with Momo—something little Momo couldn't grasp at the time—she still believed that behind her melancholic mask, Mother secretly delighted in Momo's sadness.

Looking back, Momo wasn't sure how that final, decisive surgery had begun, nor how it ended. That day, she'd thought it was just another routine examination. They anaesthetized her as usual, but when she woke up, something felt terribly wrong. Her body seemed to have undergone some changes (for instance, her pee-pee was missing), and the world around her felt strange.

Right. And Andy was gone.

When Momo realized that Andy wasn't by her side, she didn't immediately throw a tantrum. Not because the doctors had given her sedatives, but because she'd had a premonition that the grown-ups would steal Andy away from her just like they had stolen her freedom and siloed her off in a lonely dark ward. If her premonition had come true, screams of protest wouldn't do any good.

And Momo felt these huge postsurgical changes weren't limited to her missing member and Andy's mysterious disappearance. There was something else that Momo couldn't quite put her finger on . . .

In hindsight, she was too young to understand.

In her wildest dreams, she couldn't have imagined the changes she'd been through.

When she got out of the hospital and returned to her home from so long ago, Mother stayed with her for a few days and they read the encyclopedia together. But before long, Mother was rushing off to work again; she'd been promoted, of course.

Barely ten years old and alone at home, Momo found everything very dull. She stripped off her clothes and touched herself—body, breasts, belly—but her pee-pee was gone. Mother said that Andy was still with her, but where? She couldn't find her. Momo ran bare naked to the shower. The stream of water gushed onto the place where her pee-pee had been cut off, tingling agreeably. This must be what the encyclopedia had referred to as "arousal." Pity Andy wasn't there to give it a try . . .

But Andy was long gone.

Mother had made up a new bedroom for Momo to have all to herself when she got back from the hospital. Sleeping alone took some getting used to, but Momo had no choice.

"Mother! Why can't I sleep in your room? Before I went to the hospital, I always slept in your room."

"Momo, you're grown up now, and when people grow up they have to sleep by themselves."

"But in laserdisc movies, all the grown-ups sleep in pairs."

"Friends who love each other sleep together, silly. Like you and Andy used to."

She didn't want to listen to Mother. She thought Mother just envied Momo's relationship with Andy. Mother was definitely jealous of Momo!

Of course, Mother knew that Momo was bored alone at home, so she invited other children from the neighborhood over to play. But Momo didn't want to play with any of them. She only wanted Andy.

Mother herself occasionally brought a friend home, and if they got home late, Mother would let the friend sleep in her bedroom. Of course Momo wasn't allowed in. She still had to sleep in her room. Momo was enraged whenever Mother let a friend stay over. She thought of how she and Andy had been close like that—no, even closer—and now it was all gone. It was as if Mother was trying to rub it in Momo's face!

Her fury aside, though, Momo was curious: What exactly did Mother and her friends *do* in the bedroom? Did they fall asleep as soon as they lay down? Momo doubted it. Did they lie in bed whispering to each other the way Momo and Andy had? Or did they play doctor? Surely they didn't just spend all their time reading discbooks! Or did they hug and kiss like the people in the laserdisc videos?

Momo got angrier just thinking about it, and she decided to get to the bottom of it. But Mother wasn't about to open the door and let Momo in to observe, which meant Momo was going to have to spy on her. But how? She didn't have a monitor like the one at the hospital, and it wasn't like Mother was going to pick up the phone and answer Momo's prank video calls.

One night when Mother's friend Draupadi spent the night, Momo was bored out of her mind. She had no choice but to haul out the discbooks to try to relieve the monotony—but it was still unbearably tedious. Momo stopped Mother at dawn before she left for work.

"I want Andy!" This was the most frank way she could think to convey the intensity of her feelings of protest.

Mother was at a loss. She didn't know how to console Momo. All she could do was fish out a credit card emblazoned with the Mastercard logo and hand it to Momo; it was a VIP discbook rental account card.

"I can't deal with your temper tantrums! If you don't want to make new friends, then read more! Take this card and go buy some books yourself; you reject whatever I bring home for you from work anyway."

Momo grabbed the Mastercard, dissatisfied, and caught the Rapid Transit shuttle to the district shopping center.

The Rapid Transit System in this district was all aboveground, so Momo could see blue fish darting by in the rippling tide through the windows of her compartment.

What was really going on out there beyond the window?

According to the encyclopedia, the earth was like an apple. In the twentieth century, humans lived on land, which was like the waxy coating on the surface of the apple; but by the twenty-first century, they had pierced that translucent layer of wax and begun living in the space between the wax and the skin of the apple. The oceans were like a membrane of wax.

Living under the wax membrane was so depressing, thought Momo. How exciting it would be if she could just pierce the surface of the waves and emerge back up on the layer where humanity used to live, if she could breathe oxygen unfiltered by air-conditioning machines and see for herself that notorious star, the sun. . . . But in T City the law stipulated that only adults could go sightseeing on land, and even then you had to apply for a permit from the relevant authorities first, and put on cumbersome sun protection gear before surfacing from the seaway corridor. She'd overheard Mother say that there was nothing up there but ruins scattered across a barren wasteland, that the famous rainforests and grasslands would never recover. And that squadrons of guerilla M units roamed among the metallic factories and fields of solar panels, committing acts of war and terrorism on behalf of their countries. Mother couldn't understand how anyone—tourists, anthropologists, factory technicians trying to get promoted—was crazy enough to go sunbathing up there. What if you accidentally got killed by an M unit?

But little Momo understood. She had read in a discbook that in the twentieth century, there were also thrill seekers who took their chances under the ocean. If it was risky for twenty-first-century denizens of the ocean to go on land, then it was tempting fate even more for these people to move to the ocean. Momo had watched a documentary on a laserdisc once called *The Wonderful, Horrible Life of Leni Riefenstahl*, about the director Leni Riefenstahl and her life in ancient Germany under the Nazis.

After the Second World War, she was critically condemned for directing the infamous Nazi propaganda films *Triumph of the Will* and *Olympia*. But this didn't stop her from living a full life. As an old lady she was still in full possession of her faculties, and in her later years she indulged her love of deep-sea diving and underwater photography, refusing to be outdone by younger male divers. Diving into the water in her black wetsuit, Leni would bounce among the fish, effortlessly shouldering her cameras and oxygen tanks. She once stroked the tail of an enormous skate as black as a Dracula's cape without showing a trace of fear; the enigmatic beauty of deep ocean fish was revealed under her caress. Momo figured that if in the technologically backward age of the twentieth century people had the guts to move from the land to the sea, what was so frightening about going on land for people today?

Momo hoped she would get to see the surface when she was old enough. Reach out and caress the remains of a vanquished Combat M unit in the desert with her hand, and when no one was looking, secretly remove one of her sunscreen gloves so that the skin of her palm could bake in the direct scorch of the sun. To experience for just a moment the kind of trespass that her fellow citizens could never understand or forgive . . .

But young Momo, sitting there on the Rapid Transit, had never even touched real sea water. She pressed her tiny palm against the window of the compartment and looked through the glass to the protective waterproof membrane beyond it, and beyond that to the ocean.

The ocean: just a membrane on the surface of a giant apple.

When she arrived at the district shopping center, Momo passed a large patch of lawn where an artisanal lawncare technician was proudly mowing the bright green grass.

She entered the electronics store and saw a full set of Mega-Hard and Microsoft best-selling discbooks in a glass case. She wasn't particularly interested. Since Mother brought so many of them home each day, she had plenty of discbooks already. With Mother's industry connections, they already had all the newest and most popular discbooks at home—way more than the selection here in the shop. But then why even bother going to a bookstore at all? She didn't know how to feel. Momo knew she should feel lucky that her own bookshelves were fuller than those of any shop. But she was so sick of the books at home she could cry. How colorless was her young life, if even a shop full of new discbooks felt tedious.

Just as she began to feel hopeless, she caught sight of a set of new toys in a corner of the shop: "Scanners."

According to the description on the box, a scanner could gather distant images and data and then transmit them to a computer for decryption. A scanner was different from a video camera in that a scanner didn't have a lens. Instead it worked much the same way a bat uses echolocation: by emitting a radiographic pulse [NB: "bat": pre-twenty-first-century rodent-like flying mammal]. When the pulse bounced back, a high-fidelity visual rendering was produced from the data, so a scanner could capture images just like a video camera. And since scanners didn't use lenses, they were tiny enough for use in a variety of covert applications. Moreover, they were wireless and could be operated remotely from a personal computer. So scanners were great for any basic espionage. In fact, scanners were no bigger than a Band-aid and just as simple to use.

The clerk greeted Momo. "Are you looking for a scanner? Aren't they great toys?"

"Toys?" Momo felt a bit disappointed. She thought scanners were those high-tech devices she'd read about in spy novels, but it turned out they were just a children's toy!

"Well, yeah, but a fascinating toy. I don't mean 'toy' in a bad way; one of the best features of a scanner is powerful close-up imaging. Pity so many people are working hard to disable that very feature. Now lots of businesses are installing hidden jammers in their buildings so scanners can't capture trade secrets, so in some places scanners are useless. They may not be great for spies, but a scanner still makes the perfect children's toy. It's great for playing cops and robbers."

"I'll take two."

Momo took out the Mastercard Mother gave her but asked the clerk not to itemize the receipt.

"Don't list 'scanner' on the receipt. Since it's a toy, just write 'computer game' on the receipt."

Momo didn't want Mother to see it.

Ten-year-old Momo waited by the computer for images captured by her scanner to appear onscreen.

She'd purchased two scanners. Toys they might be, but they were also smart machines, and weren't cheap.

Before Mother left for work that day, Momo stuck one of the scanners on her briefcase, and then when she left, she placed the other one on the corner of the desk in Mother's bedroom. Momo wanted to observe a day in the life of her mother.

But as soon as Mother left the house, the scanner on her briefcase stopped working, transmitting only static. It was just like the clerk at the electronics store had said: major corporations all over T City had installed jammers to prevent spying. The scanner's "antenna" would never reach MegaHard offices. But on the other hand, the bedroom scanner functioned perfectly and had a scope of 180 degrees. From her own room, Momo could watch images transmitted from Mother's bedroom with just a nimble flick of the mouse, achieving the same effect as a miniature camera. The image it transmitted was crystal clear. With the close-up function, Momo could even see a curly hair left on the coverlet.

When Mother got home that night, she brought Draupadi over for dinner. Momo had seen her several times before.

Though Momo hated that Mother neglected her when she had a friend over, she didn't mind Draupadi. Draupadi was trim, with luminescent black skin. Momo heard she was Indian, and when she looked her up later in "Who's Who," she learned that the name came from the ancient Hindu text known as the Mahabharata. Momo thought Draupadi was gorgeous. It was a long while before Momo realized that she had seen Draupadi before, back when she was in the hospital and had mistaken her for one of the doctors. Momo hadn't seen an adult this handsome in a very long time. But she didn't praise Draupadi's attributes to Mother. She felt wronged: Momo had lost Andy, but here was Mother with such a lovely playmate!

Draupadi treated Momo very warmly over dinner, but as soon as the adults finished eating, they retreated to Mother's bedroom to talk. They told Momo to go off and entertain herself with some discbooks,. . . But Momo wanted to shred the discbooks one by one with her teeth! The cold discbooks were her only lousy company!

Momo skulked to her room with a pout and turned on her computer, randomly picking out a disc. But it was another Shakespearean tragedy! She was so angry she couldn't finish it. She felt like lonely Hamlet—all alone in the hospital ward, though at least in the hospital she'd had Andy to keep her company. But Andy had disappeared; and returning home she'd thought Mother would stay with her, but that wasn't true.

Was she meant to have only computers and discs for company for the rest of her life? Not only was Mother absent, she had found herself her Indian friend. Momo remembered that in the hospital, Mother would only occasionally look in on her via the ward monitors or video call.

Good thing she'd installed the scanner. Momo would be able to see whatever it was that Mother and Draupadi were getting up to in the bedroom!

She booted up the scanner with a tap of the keyboard . . . only to find Mother's bedroom completely empty. Though the scanner had a wide-angle scope, inevitably there were blind spots. Mother and Draupadi probably were standing just outside the scanner's range. But Momo's scanner was pointed directly at the bed in the middle of the room. Surely they couldn't avoid it forever?

Before long Draupadi entered the frame. She was dressed a little differently now: she'd pulled her hair into a ponytail, and she'd changed out of the dark blue *qipao* she'd been wearing and into something form-fitting and white as snow. Soon Mother entered the frame. She was completely naked.

Momo clapped quietly. At last she would find out all the good things Mother and her friend were doing!

It had been a very long time since she'd seen Mother naked— she was a bit plumper than Momo remembered. Momo used the scanner to zoom in on the triangle of black hair between Mother's legs and saw that she didn't have a pee-pee either. [Momo saw] Mother, framed by the close-up, squared her shoulders and sat on the bed like a buddha. Draupadi whispered something in Mother's ear.

Pity that Momo couldn't listen in. The scanner couldn't pick up sound; it only captured images.

In the frame Draupadi spread a big blue-black cloth out on the bed, which Mother then lay on, face down. Mother was facing the scanner, her eyes closed. She looked relaxed. Draupadi's dark fingers fluttered across the delicate white skin of Mother's back, kneading gently with a semitranslucent creamy yellow ointment. Mother said something, her eyes still closed.

But Momo's pleasure at her successful spying mission quickly gave way to jealousy.

Why did Mother get to play these relaxing games with her friend, while Momo could only spy in secret from the other room?

While watching secretly from the other room, Momo noticed a pair of eyes returning her gaze: the black and white of Draupadi's eyes looked intently back at her from her computer screen. Momo was startled, terrified that Draupadi had discovered the scanner spying on her. She hurriedly changed the scanner's viewing angle and turned off the close-up function. But Draupadi just turned her head so that she was still looking directly at Momo. Had Draupadi really detected the inconspicuous little scanner? And yet her expression was not irritated or angry. Rather her eyes seemed to say: I know you're watching me . . . and so, respectfully, I return your gaze. Momo immediately turned the scanner off. She recalled reading the foreword to a horror story called *Misery*, by Stephen King, in which the author quoted Nietzsche: "When you look into the abyss . . . the abyss also looks into you."

But Momo couldn't contain her curiosity. She turned the scanner back on. So what if the people in the room figured out what she was up to? What would they do? The image of Mother appeared again on Momo's computer. Mother still lay blissfully prone on the bed, and Draupadi still stood to one side, massaging Mother's back while staring directly into the scanner. Draupadi said something to Mother, then approached the scanner . . . but didn't remove it. From her computer screen, Momo watched as Draupadi turned on the 3-D Hi-Fi HDTV Unit at the base of the bed . . . and then all she saw was static.

It was obvious that Draupadi had deliberately jammed the scanner: she'd seen it. Would she tell Mother?

At the time, Momo thought that she'd been witness to some great secret. But she hadn't considered: if the briefcase scanner had been jammed so that all she saw was static, then what about the scanner in Mother's room? Why wasn't it jammed too? If Mother was such a critical employee at a major corporation, wouldn't the company also take care to protect both her public and private lives? Wouldn't the house have been outfitted with jammers as well? The image transmitted from Mother's room was crystal clear.

But just because an image is clear doesn't mean you can trust it. It could have been manipulated.

It was only later that Momo began to doubt the scanner's fidelity. She could hardly trust her own eyes, let alone the eyes of a machine!

Which begged the question: If that was true, then what about the eyes of androids, which were part flesh and part machine? Could those be trusted?

Momo turned off the scanner and inserted an encyclopedia. She wanted to know exactly what Draupadi and Mother had been doing.

As it turned out, Draupadi was a dermal care technician! A famous one.

It later dawned on Momo that it wasn't unreasonable for Mother to bring a dermal care technician home so often: Mother's job meant that she had to keep up a pleasing appearance.

Paying someone to help with her dermal maintenance regime was only natural.

Draupadi left as soon as it was light out, and Mother rushed out for work. Momo was left at home by herself again.

Sigh. Another dreary day! Momo wasn't content to stay in her room. She had fully recovered by now, so she decided to go play in the district park. It was windy out, and Momo could feel the chill on her skin. She had a brainwave: she'd borrow one of Mother's hats. So she dashed back to Mother's unlocked room.

The bedspread on Mother's bed was crisp, clean, and pulled taut, without even a wrinkle or stray hair. Had Draupadi really given Mother a massage last night? If so, there was no trace.

The gluestrip with the scanner was also missing from the corner of the desk. Had Draupadi torn it off? Did Mother know what was going on? But something else caught Momo's eye . . .

Mother's palm-sized notebook computer lay on the desk. Mother had forgotten to take it with her.

Momo knew that Mother used it to record all sorts of things, like bank account details, diary entries, and her work calendar. Odd that she had left it at home. Normally Mother would go off in a corner at home, lost in thought as she wrote in her diary, but she would never let Momo see the diary's contents.

But now the notebook computer had fallen into Momo's hands. If she wanted to know all of Mother's secrets, all she had to do was open it and look!

Momo opened the device, which was emblazoned with the MegaHard logo. It was unlocked!

"Enter your password."

Password? How would Momo know Mother's password?

Mother's password was several digits long. Momo had no clue what they were.

Momo entered her birthday, June 6, 2070, or "20700606," but got an error message. Next she tried Mother's birthday: December 24, 2050 ("20501224"). Wrong again. Maybe the password wasn't even numbers. Was it in English? So she entered "I love Andy" . . . which of course didn't work either.

A message appeared on the screen:

"Three invalid login attempts. Notebook is now locked."

The words then disappeared from the screen.

That was no fun! Momo hadn't seen a thing. She might as well go to the park.

Momo wiped her fingerprints off the notebook with a paper towel. If Mother figured out that she'd tried to look in her notebook, she'd be furious.

She picked out the smallest cap from Mother's wardrobe, put it on her head, and fled out the door.

She hadn't been to the park in a very long time, since before the hospital. She loved playing on the swing and feeling the gust of air beneath her skirt.

She ran into the park. It was early morning so there was hardly anyone there . . . but someone was already sitting in her favorite swing. An adult. The adult saw Momo approaching and said nothing, just watched her attentively with a faint smile.

It was a man.

Momo sat down on a swing next to the man, and he kept gazing at her. Momo recalled reading two entries in the encyclopedia on "Pedophile" and "Sexual Harassment."

Momo gave him a sly look and said:

"Did you know that I used to have a pee-pee? But now I don't."

"Oh?"

"Do you want to touch under my skirt and see?"

The man hesitated, but then did it.

Momo felt a familiar, agreeable tingle. And the man's hand was gentler than the showerhead had been. The man looked into her eyes with a rapt expression. At first Momo thought she might bite his hand or kick him in the groin, or maybe scream—that's what the discbooks had instructed her to do. But she didn't resist. She didn't feel like resisting, because that would feel mean, and besides, she also felt the thrill of revenge. Exactly whom she was getting this revenge on, however, she wasn't sure . . .

"Why don't you have one?" asked the man.

"I had an operation."

"Oh."

"Hey, want to pull down your pants and show me your weenie? Nobody's around, so you don't have to be shy." This made Momo feel even more wicked.

"I don't have a weenie."

"Why not? You look like a man."

"I'm actually a cyborg. I'm a kind of robot that's been designed to look like a real person. My skin and hair are no different than those of a real person, but I'm not a man—I was custom-made by my owner, modeled on his younger self. I only left the factory a month ago."

CYBORG.

Momo had seen that entry in the encyclopedia but had never read it carefully.

"You're a cyborg?"

"Have you heard of them? People usually call me 'Andy,' which is short for 'Android,' which is similar to a cyborg."

Momo understood, and her legs began to tremble. So "Andy" meant "Android." Cyborg.

"What's your name?" asked Andy.

"My name is Momo . . . and you're Andy? Don't you have any other names?"

"No. As soon as I left the factory, humans dubbed me 'Andy.' My owner didn't give me a unique name, but he couldn't just call me by my 10-digit serial number, right? Calling cyborgs 'Andy' has kind of become a convention at this point. It's like with robot dogs: white-coated ones are called "Whitey" and spotted ones are called "Spot." Pretty boring. Whenever I think about how every day there are androids joining society who have the same name as me, I feel slighted. Why can't humans just give us more unique names? At least it would make our short time on earth slightly more interesting."

This Andy was very talkative, and the more Momo listened to him chatter on and on, the less she focused on the vague discomfort rising in her chest . . .

"Take your name: 'Momo.' It's so silly. It sounds . . . yummy."

Even though she felt a profound sadness, this made her laugh. "Why?"

"When you eat a peach you make a 'nom nom' sound! And when you eat a tasty mushroom soup. And when my owner kisses his lover, it's 'nom nom' for most of the day! The lips and tongue must taste delicious."

"You're fascinating, Andy . . ." Momo didn't feel quite comfortable saying the name. The rightful owner of the name was a young girl who'd gone missing, not a whole pack of cyborgs Momo had never met.

"Momo! I love this park and come here a lot, but I've never seen you here before."

Momo nodded. She didn't have the energy to elaborate.

Big Andy had only come out of the factory a month ago, which was when Momo had been stuck in the hospital ward.

Playing in the park was something she'd only done before going to the hospital. The swing that Andy sat in used to be Momo's favorite—it went the highest.

Andy added, "Last night my owner stayed at his lover's house, so when I woke up this morning I was all alone. It was so boring, so I came to the park. And I thought if I don't play now, I may never get the chance again. Tomorrow I'm having surgery too."

"Why?"

"Transplant. My owner thinks his body is falling apart. His belly is squishy and saggy, so he wants to use my body instead. Which means that in the hospital they will cut out the parts he doesn't want from his body and replace them with parts from my body. Afterward, my owner and I will be one." The android chuckled. "But he's going to keep his original plumbing, to serve those young boys always chasing after him. He says it feels more genuine and intimate that way. So there's no need for replacement parts there, haha."

When Momo got home that day, she immediately stripped off her clothes and looked at her naked body in the mirror. It felt both strange and familiar.

Flustered, she put her clothes back on, then a thick overcoat, and then wrapped herself in a comforter, as if to forget there was a body attached beneath her skull. She understood what was happening, but she didn't quite know how to face it. Back when Mother said that Andy was still with Momo and would always be with Momo, did she mean that Andy's body and her body had been spliced together? Did these two hands belong to Momo or to Andy? Whose belly was this? She didn't have a pee-pee, so that delicate flesh below her belly button must have belonged to Andy! There were no scars, so there was no way to tell which parts had been added on. What about her fingers? Were they Andy's too? Momo had bitten off Andy's middle finger . . . Momo puzzled over it but couldn't put it all together.

When Mother got home from work, Momo whined; she didn't know where to start, so she just started begging again for her Andy to come back. Though she understood now that there was more than one Andy [out there], her heart was set on one Andy in particular. . . .

"Bring Andy back!" It was another direct and clear protest, and she voiced it loud and clear. But Mother thought she was just trying to provoke her.

"Momo, do you have any idea how much it cost to custom order a completely sterile, sentient cyborg and perform such a perfect, scar-free procedure?"

Then Mother solemnly explained to Momo. "Andy's flesh was specially designed to grow in tandem with your own, to undergo biological changes along with your own. It was the most advanced kind of cyborg available. The hospital specifically designed her to keep you company and ensure that you got used to her body and didn't reject her. You should be very happy with the surgery, since you liked Andy so much."

"Andy isn't with me! She's gone! You murdered her! You dismembered her, like in a murder mystery! It's murder!"

"Momo, you have no idea how much this surgery cost . . ."

"I don't care! Quit telling me I don't understand, I understand more than you think! You think I don't understand *Hamlet*, but I've read *Merchant of Venice*! Don't think I don't understand! I know you killed Andy!"

"Enough, Momo!"

But Momo didn't stop. She was on a roll now, and she let loose a torrent of abuse:

"You're the most selfish person alive! You stole my friend! You're free to make friends and bring them into your bedroom and take off your clothes and touch each other all you want!"

She ran into her room and slammed the door. She tried to vent her anger by playing a video game, but when the MegaHard logo appeared on the screen she turned it off in a rage.

She ran out of her room, ready to scream at Mother some more, but . . .

Mother was nowhere to be found. And she didn't come home all night.

Momo woke the next morning even angrier and more exasperated than she'd been the night before. Without checking if Mother had come home or not, she just returned to the park. The male Andy was already there on the swing.

Momo stepped forward to sit next to him. In her rush to leave the park the day before, she had forgotten her cap. It wasn't his fault.

"Momo, you look upset."

"You remind me of a different Andy. She was a girl the same age as me."

"So she must have been made custom? She must have been really cute. What was her name?"

"She was called Andy too . . ."

Momo struggled to say it out loud: a name she so cherished, that felt entirely unique to her, was in fact basically a product name.

"Oh," said Andy, looking just a little disappointed. "Just like me."

"Mother told me that me and my Andy are already together in one body."

"A lot of Andys are designed to be joined with their owners. Like me. Designed custom to match our owners' measurements."

"Hey, isn't your surgery today?"

"It's this afternoon. So this is my last chance to play on the swing. Once I've been joined with my owner, he definitely won't come to play here. All he cares about is going to bars and spas to meet boys . . ." As he was speaking, something dawned on him. "Of course! After a full-body transplant, my owner will have a much nicer figure, so he'll finally have something to show off in the spas!"

"Who is your owner?"

"His name is Paolo. He's the best weed removal technician in the district."

A hint of pride played across Big Andy's face.

In the twenty-first-century Asia Pacific, grass and trees were exceedingly rare and costly, so professional garden maintenance workers were considered highly skilled and respected professionals. Only wealthy people could afford to have gardens, so only a select few could afford to hire a weed removal technician. So anyone who could afford to custom order a cyborg was either a new-age yuppie like a weed removal technician or a workaholic like Momo's mother.

Momo had seen Big Andy's weed removal technician. He was a young-looking guy who weeded the garden outside the District Committee's Office with great dexterity, his large feet planted squarely on the emerald-green lawn. Stepping on the grass was a privilege restricted to weed removal technicians. Momo recalled he was indeed a little plump, his belly sticking out as he mowed the grass.

"I know him. But he doesn't look old at all. Why does he want surgery? Mother says that young people concerned with their looks really just need to see a dermal care technician for younger, more elastic skin."

"Silly girl. Skin care can only fix superficial problems; it's no good for internal problems. Ordinarily my owner would see a dermal care technician, but his body is no good due to some problem in his belly. Do you know what an M unit is?"

Momo nodded.

Model M units were hot children's toys right now. Momo didn't particularly like playing with them, but she knew what they were.

The "M" in "M unit" referred to the legendary wanderer, the Monkey King Sun Wukong, from ancient Chinese lore. The first working prototype for the M unit was a kind of advanced, semi-automated android produced by a Chinese engineer named Tang. The prototype was deemed "The Wandering Monkey" for its extreme agility and its assault functions, which were precisely what Sun Wukong needed to escort his Master safely to the Western States. The nickname also referred to the M unit's ability to be customized according to a client's specifications (just like Sun Wukong's ability to shape-shift into seventy-two different forms).

You could say that cyborgs lay somewhere between human and machine, while the M unit lay somewhere between cyborg and robot. M units had basic artificial intelligence, but they were made from more heavy-duty, robotlike material.

"Then why don't I use M units as an example?" Andy continued. "If the surface of an M unit is damaged, all you have to do to repair it is add a new layer of protective membrane over the varnish on the hull; but if there's a problem with the mechanics, then it will need a complete rebuild. You might have to replace half of the entire unit's parts. I mention the example of an M unit because of its similarities to the human body: you can repair the human body's external flaws just by seeing a dermal care technician, but internal problems call for surgery, like major organ transplant, where it's best for the organ to come from another human being. But the death rate for humans is too low, so there aren't enough organ donors. Plus, most of these donatable organs are reserved for people with serious illnesses, not for people like my owner who just want them for cosmetic reasons. So the simplest solution is to order a custom-made cyborg. Then you can replace any body part you want."

"But if that's true, doesn't the cyborg disappear in the process? Aren't you scared?"

"I don't have a choice. Our fates are decided entirely by the wealthy, powerful people who commission us. We don't have a say in the matter." Andy shrugged. "Besides, cyborgs like me are purpose-built entirely to replenish our owners' parts, not to be companions. The short time I get to spend with my owner is meant to get him used to me. After all, I'm going to become his heart, liver, flesh, and blood, so he should spend some time with me . . ."

His eyes grew red. "Of course I don't want to leave this world. But when I think how this very afternoon I will be inside my owner's body, I remember those lyrics: 'There is you in me, there is me in you . . .' I guess I should be crying tears of joy . . ."

"Will I still be able to see you?"

"When you see the top weed removal specialist in the district, you'll be seeing me. By then I will be entirely within him."

Momo thought of a big question.

"But will I still be able to hear you?"

"I don't know—"

Andy's face grew pale. "My owner will control speech. I'll just provide organs for him to choose from—"

It had been such a long time since Momo had spoken with her Andy.

Mother had told her that Andy's body was within her own.
And this Andy confirmed it. Momo loved being with Andy, but
not like this. She loved the togetherness of reading with Andy,
but even if she was now reading literally through Andy's eyes, it
could never compare to that feeling of togetherness. And she had
loved hearing Andy talk, hearing the sound of her voice. Now,
even though she and Andy had been fully merged—like coffee
with coffee creamer, where she was the coffee and Andy was the
powder—she couldn't talk with her anymore.

Coffee might taste different when you add cream, but it's
still coffee. But the powdered cream . . . when you sprinkle it
in, it dissolves completely. Could Andy speak through Momo's
mind?

After her surgery, a voice sometimes emerged from deep
inside her. Was this an aftereffect of the surgery, or was Andy
murmuring in there?

For example, after her surgery, Momo began to hear fragments of melodies too discordant to reproduce and see flashes of
complex images she couldn't describe. Had Andy died inside her?
Was Momo's body an android grave, the spectral voice of Andy's
spirit echoing in her mind?

Momo dreamt of an ice-cold house under a starry sky, the
ceaseless drone of silvery chrome machines, the mirror finish of
gleaming white gears. Now she realized it matched male Andy's
description of a munitions depot up on the surface.

"I can't stay and chat. I have to get ready for the operating
table."

"I hope the surgery goes well."

"Momo, I hope I see you again. I'll try to get my owner to
greet you sometime . . ."

Momo gripped the swing cables tightly. The wind rustled
under her skirt, where no undergarments stopped it from entering

her large intestine and penetrating deep within her small intestine until she felt the chill all the way in her stomach, like it was snowing in there, the snowflakes covering Andy's corpse.

When it got dark, she went home. Mother was there, but she remained completely silent.

From that moment on, mother and daughter exchanged very few words. They didn't speak at all unless it was absolutely necessary.

Mother offered no objections when Momo asked to go to school far away.

"I want to study skin care arts. I want to become a professional dermal care technician. Once I've finished my studies, I'll pay you back for tuition and living expenses, with interest."

Again Mother raised no objections.

And sure enough, when Momo turned twenty-five, had won an award, and was earning lots of money, she deposited a huge sum with MegaHard. Mother responded right away with an email. But it was only a receipt and nothing more.

After moving away to boarding school, Momo never saw Mother again. Once she had graduated and was busy with her practice, she only ever saw Mother's face when it appeared in MegaHard ads for new discbooks.

As for Paolo's Andy (now that he'd gotten his wish and become part of the weed removal technician's body, she just thought of him as "Paolo's Andy"), Momo never saw him again, because she never returned to play on the swings at the park, nor even to visit the neighborhood from her childhood.

Before the weed removal technician died, had he ever been back to the park?

She had no idea.

\* \* \*

Momo learned about the weed removal technician's death when she was browsing the online news at boarding school one day.

The headline read: "History Repeating Itself? Paolo Pasolini Dies a Horrible Death!"

It turned out that the weed removal technician had been deliberately mowed down by a car, which then ran back and forth over his head until his entire skull had been crushed and shattered so thoroughly that even the most biotechnologically advanced surgeries couldn't save him. For an automated surgery to be successful, you needed at the very least a living human brain.

Why would someone do such a horrifically cruel thing?

The controversial details came out in the news: the profligate middle-aged weed removal technician and fading beauty— known as Paolo—had spent wads of cash on a cyborg, and then lost vast sums pursuing love among the district's "rough trade." After an especially messy breakup, one of these young toughs raped Paolo, smashed a bottle on his head, and then crushed his skull under the wheels of his car. And that was the end of the Lothario weed removal specialist.

Was the demise of the weed removal specialist at the hands of his paramour a cause for celebration or for righteous rage? Some people would argue that it's better to die in the heat of passion than to die in some ordinary way; Paolo was a passionate artist who probably had no regrets. If you wanted to be an artist, you had to look death in the face.

It was Paolo's Andy who Momo cared about. Paolo's Andy had died for his owner's lovemaking. Was this a source of pride and joy for the cyborg? She doubted it. Paolo's Andy had died for his owner, but was his owner thinking of his cyborg when his skull was about to be crushed to smithereens? Sorry to say, he was probably thinking of the young man who raped him!

Besides, Paolo's Andy had died long ago, well before the car incident. Andy sacrificed his independence the minute he became one with Paolo, all so Paolo could be more attractive. If that was the case, then Andy's second death didn't really count . . . though possibly it had been even more terrifying than the first. This second death meant the cyborg's devotion, his selflessness, was all in vain. Crushed to bits.

Momo couldn't help but think about her own Andy inside her. What apologies could she offer her, what words of gratitude? She existed because of Andy's death. She was like a birdcage with canary Andy locked inside; the canary didn't sing and it didn't fly. It was like a corpse was living inside her.

Momo lived alone with her birdcage, later taking in a small dog. She could only bear it because she believed that dogs—unlike cats—don't eat birds. Or at least those were the rules handed down from the twentieth century.

So she thought.

Between 2080 and 2090, while she was attending boarding school, Momo lived very simply, even as Mother rose through the ranks of a publishing empire. She had no desire to rely on Mother, with one exception: industrious as she was, Momo had no choice but to use the many great books published by MegaHard.

Mother worked herself to the bone for MegaHard; she personally handled all aspects of major business transactions. So much so that once Momo turned on her computer screen only to see Mother's face leap out at her, playing the lead role in an ad for the encyclopedia. Twenty-first-century computers were like televisions in the twentieth century, and every few minutes an ad would appear. Even in movie theaters, which had all but gone extinct, Momo saw Mother's advertisements for encyclopedias. Once during a craze for all things retro, she had gone to an Italian-style cinema called the Nuovo Cinema Paradiso to see a vintage Northern European period piece, Ingmar Bergman's *Autumn Sonata*. On the screen, the corners of Mother's lips turned up in a friendly, maternal smile as her career at MegaHard took off. Momo left the theater alone and returned to the space between her computer console and her massage table.

Meanwhile, Momo got really good with her fingers. During her practice labs at Beauty School she used all ten at once: first for massage, then to apply skin creams, and finally to massage the nutritive creams deep into muscle tissue. Even when she was using her personal computer, her fingers never left the keyboard as she wrote up her homework, surfed the internet, typed e-mails, or read discbooks. She was a serious, hardworking student.

And she was a serious girl. One night when she was fifteen, Momo placed her fingers in the basin between her legs and played there the kind of sonata that you can't play by day. Losing herself in blissful massage, she imagined riding a bubble up to the surface of the earth and felt the soles of her feet land upon scorching dry yellow shards of gravel. Here she began to gently stroke the scattered pieces of an M unit felled in battle, bloodless remains that had survived the relentless baptism of sunlight, and then—moved by the M unit's fate—Momo fantasized that she was touching its face . . . only to discover it was Andy's face.

Oh. So the M unit and Andy were both cyborgs . . . Andy was a cyborg, not a human.

Was Andy even born, did she even die?

At this point Momo woke from her wild masturbatory reverie, unable to continue.

She needed a shower. To scrub away these random fragments of thought. She stripped off her clothes and stood beneath the showerhead, touching her body through the lather. This beautiful young body, her torso so smooth and free of scars that it was as if no surgery had ever been performed on it. But was it? Her body? Did it belong to her? Or to Andy? If Andy's transplanted organs could grow and age along with her body, did that mean that Momo's emerging breasts concealed glands that belonged to Andy? Andy couldn't reproduce, so Momo had never gotten her period. . . . These breasts, her lower body . . . whose were they?

Momo couldn't help but wonder if, after the transplant, Andy had become part of Momo or it was Momo who had become some piece of Andy's flesh. Her surgery had been a major procedure, transferring a great deal of Andy's tissue and nerves to Momo's body. But how much? What percentage? Surely not more than 99 percent?

Postsurgery, was Momo really just left with her head and her brain—containing her memories—while the rest of the body came from Andy?

That couldn't be true, could it? She loved Andy, but this wasn't how she wanted to be "with" her.

Momo was like a canary locked inside a beautiful cage.

# 7

"What an exceptional name you've chosen, 'Salon Canary.' I'm sure your technique is just as lovely," commented Draupadi. "I'm curious—who does 'canary' refer to? What does it mean?"

Draupadi showed up out of the blue at Momo's salon right after it opened. Momo had turned twenty-five that year—it was 2095—by which time she had already established guidelines for her practice: she would take skin care clients by prior appointment only, and she would flatly refuse any drop-ins. But when Draupadi showed up, she couldn't turn her away. Draupadi was the first dermal care technician Momo had ever known, her elder. If Draupadi hadn't turned up years ago, Momo might never have taken this path.

"Momo, I haven't seen you in so many years. Do you remember me? Your face is still as pretty as a peach, but it's gotten rosier with age."

Draupadi wore a sari of violet and indigo, and inexplicably carried a small violin case like one of those old-time cases terrorists used to conceal machine guns. Draupadi hadn't aged a bit; her nice figure and gleaming dark complexion were exactly as Momo remembered. She was an established dermal care technician, after all, so she took good care of herself. Having only just opened her own business, Momo thought perhaps it was her own lack of self-confidence that made her notice Draupadi's arrogant self-assurance. Momo almost couldn't look directly at her.

Draupadi entered the salon and without another word, put down her violin case and made herself right at home. She was petite, so at first it looked like she was only wearing one loose-fitting purple sari, but when she removed it, there was another deep indigo sari beneath.

Momo was startled, but Draupadi smiled and said, "I'm wearing too much clothing, aren't I? Do you know why I'm called 'Draupadi'?"

Draupadi removed her second layer of clothing, and sure enough, underneath there was a third layer of pale blue, which she then removed to reveal a fourth layer in green. This was followed by yellow, then orange. The seventh layer was red, and when she removed that, Draupadi's naked body finally appeared. It reminded Momo of a novel from the twentieth century called *If on a Winter's Night a Traveler*, in which a young girl wears many layers of clothing and assumes a new identity every time she removes one. "Are you thinking of Calvino's *If on a Winter's Night a Traveler*? It's not the same; I haven't changed my identity. Whether I'm wearing clothes or not, I'm still Draupadi. My name comes from the old Indian epic, the Mahabharata, have you heard of it? In the story, Draupadi wears a sari of infinite layers, so even if someone wanted to strip her clothing off, they couldn't."

Draupadi sat naked on the massage table. She seemed so thin when she was fully clothed, but her nakedness revealed the subtle fullness of her figure. Her dark skin seemed to breathe in oxygen through its very pores, lending it a supple vibrancy, a silky resilience.

"But," asked Momo boldly as she took in Draupadi's perky breasts, "haven't you just stripped naked?"

"In the Mahabharata, Draupadi wears an infinite sari because she was forced to. But I am naked now because I choose to be."

Momo worked hard playing the most complex melody on the instrument of Draupadi's body, not daring to miss a beat. She massaged vigorously, applying a meticulous concoction of algae cream to every nook and cranny. Momo was like a newly minted pianist facing a piano that was itself the living incarnation of her most revered master pianist.

She couldn't help but be reminded of Bergman's *Autumn Sonata*, which she'd seen when she was still a student. In the film the mother is a renowned pianist, but when her daughter, who is studying piano, comes of age, she must play for her mother. Since her audience is both a pianist and her mother, she plays her heart out, until she almost can't go on. That's how Momo felt, but in her case the piano, the string section, and the audience were all mixed together in one body.

Draupadi lay on the table as if intoxicated beneath Momo's skillful fingers—she kept her eyes closed and didn't say a word, only letting out an occasional groan that sounded like the pop of a balloon or the pure, quivering joy of a bubble bursting. Momo recognized the blissful expression on Draupadi's face as the same expression Mother wore back when Momo used her scanner to spy on Draupadi massaging Mother's naked body. . . . Would Draupadi bring up the spying incident with Momo? Momo didn't want to think about it. Her childhood mischief was so embarrassing.

When the two-hour-long dermal care process had been completed, Draupadi sat up and opened her eyes as if waking from a beautiful dream. She had enjoyed herself to the fullest, and said she wanted to offer Momo something priceless as compensation. She stood up, still naked, but didn't hurry to put her clothes back on. Instead she picked up the violin case. When she opened it, naturally it did not contain an instrument. But it wasn't a gun either. Rather it was a set of tubes filled with liquid, like tubes of toothpaste—skin care lotion, Momo thought. And there was an IC chip.

"I bet you thought I had an instrument or a weapon in this case. Well, these are like musical instruments. And they are also like weapons."

Draupadi took out a tube of the lotion, squeezed some into her palm, and proceeded to apply it evenly to her whole body. When she was done, Draupadi's whole body grew pale and her skin began to peel away. . . .

Like a snake from the animal encyclopedia shedding its skin, Draupadi peeled a semitranslucent layer of exuviae from her body, like a skin balloon in the shape of her body.

"I've removed another layer of clothing. So how can you be sure that I was naked just now?" Draupadi's gaze was fierce with meaning. "This is my second skin, my 'membrane skin.' It's called M skin."

These strange emulsions in the violin case were Draupadi's congratulatory gift for the grand opening of Salon Canary.

"Momo, this is a next-generation body scanner. You played with a scanner when you were little, remember? So I'm sure you'll enjoy this grown-up version—this one is designed for body play."

Draupadi's words were pregnant with meaning, as though she knew everything!

"You can't find this kind of scanner even on the black market. Insert this IC chip into your computer, and I'll teach you how to read the body."

Just before she left, Draupadi asked after Mother.

"Have the two of you seen each other lately?"

"Not so often . . ." Momo hadn't seen her mother since leaving for boarding school. In fact, the last time she'd seen her face it was in an ad for MegaHard.

"Please tell her I said hello."

Draupadi never visited Momo's salon again. Along with the scanner, she left Momo a complete set of highly concentrated emulsions, M skin fluids, and peels that had to be greatly diluted before application, so she had enough to last many years.

Thinking back on it, Momo figured Draupadi had only given her these miraculous gifts because of her friendship with Mother. So she didn't know whether to feel pleased or resentful. Didn't this just mean she was once again living in her mother's shadow?

Shadows, Momo thought. Everywhere.

Meanwhile, unknowable shadows continued to close in on Momo's unknowable body.

# 8

All right. At last this complicated backstory has reached a turning point. Here's where things get interesting.

Mother was going to visit on the day of Momo's thirtieth birthday, and Momo couldn't help but laugh—bitterly, coldly, foolishly.

Had Mother finally gotten in touch about repairing their relationship only because of Tomie Ito's damning disczine report? To safeguard her matronly public image? Was she coming to see Momo or Momo's transplanted finger? If she wanted to see her daughter so much, why had it taken her twenty years to make it happen?

In 2094, Momo turned twenty-four and won the Creative Dermal Care Aesthetics Prize for the Asia-Pacific region. It was her shining moment. As she approached the podium amid the glare of innumerable flashes, all eyes were trained on her and her prize-winning creation—the girl she'd transformed into a canary. And Mother? She'd just been promoted to president of direct marketing at MegaHard. Was she at the awards ceremony? Momo sincerely doubted it. Perhaps Mother didn't even know her daughter had won an award. Otherwise why would Momo's inbox be packed full of congratulations, while Mother had not sent a single measly e-mail? And in 2095, when Momo turned twenty-five and opened Salon Canary? Even Draupadi showed up to congratulate her, but Momo saw no sign of Mother. . . . She never imagined the busy cultural figure and president of MegaHard's direct marketing division wouldn't pay her a visit until her thirtieth birthday!

Hysterical protests darted through Momo's mind. She knew her weaning period had gone on far too long, but there was absolutely no way it was her fault.

When a child failed to detach from the parent in a timely fashion, were the obsessive behaviors and arrested development the child's fault? Or was the mother to blame, for overindulging her? Or maybe the responsibility lay with neither the child nor the mother.

What was so wrong with not weaning a child? Why force a child to grow up? If a child refused, why place blame on anyone? Why not just not grow up?

Why did such a tyrannical social imperative exist in the first place?

Mother was finally arriving. Momo felt as apprehensive as she had about her surgery back when she was ten, only this time the thing she was anxious about would happen in the blink of an eye . . .

Mother told her in an e-mail that she could find the place herself. No need to send someone to pick her up.

Momo figured this was just as well; she didn't want to reveal any weakness to Mother involuntarily.

Mother arrived at the door of her infinity-symbol-shaped salon.

Momo saw her on the monitor before she even came in, and for a moment she was dumbfounded. It was definitely Mother, but she'd aged considerably since the last time Momo saw her. So twenty years had passed after all, she thought.

But neither was the woman Momo saw on the monitor the self-possessed and graceful figure she'd seen in advertisements. The rims of her eyes were red.

Was it possible she'd been crying?

Because Momo was certainly shaken. She felt time fold in on itself, as if it wasn't 2100 anymore, and she was no longer thirty years old; suddenly it was 2080 and she was ten. A gentle terror welled up in her brain, like déjà vu. She'd felt something similar when she'd left the hospital that day when she was ten. Her surgery had been successful, Andy was gone, and Momo finally moved from the antiseptic ward to a regular hospital room to wait to be discharged. The day she was discharged, Momo lay on the white sheets of the hospital bed watching as her mother, who had carved out time in her busy schedule to escort Momo home, approached in slow motion. Mother's eyes were wet that day too.

*Momo, we can go home now,* Mother said. *You haven't been home in so very, very long.*

Mother rang the doorbell, then she pushed the door open and came in.

The woman who came in the door was the same person she'd seen on the monitor. She was dressed simply, unlike her domineering media persona. Except the rims of her eyes were neither red nor moist with tears. Had Momo's eyes been playing tricks on her?

It had been so long since they'd seen each other that for a moment neither of them knew what to say.

Just as it was getting awkward, the normally quiet little dog Andy began barking furiously at Mother.

Momo rushed to calm the little dog. "Shhhh, Andy. Behave. This is Momo's mother."

And Mother said:

"Momo . . ."

(Momo almost thought Mother was going to say: *Momo, we can go home now. You haven't been home in so very, very long.*)

But Mother said, "Momo, is your little dog named Andy too?"

Talking about the little dog relieved some of the awkwardness.

"So the dog's name is really Andy? Momo, it's so silly that you never let her go. But look at you, you're all grown up. I'm thrilled."

But after chatting about the dog, the two fell silent. Like there was nothing else to say.

"Momo, how's your finger doing?"

"Great. It hasn't impacted my work."

"That's good then."

Another awkward silence.

"Momo, what made you decide to get a dog?"

"It was a gift from one of my clients." Then she added, "She's a wealthy Japanese journalist."

"A Japanese journalist? Wow!"

"Mother, how come you made time to see me today?"

"Momo, today's your thirtieth birthday . . ."

"But I've had other birthdays. Last year I turned twenty-nine, before that twenty-five, before that fifteen. Why didn't you come see me then? Why wait until I turned thirty?"

"Momo, Mother has had some . . . difficulties . . . that prevented me from seeing you sooner."

"It's because you're so busy at work, right? I know you're a big shot in the cultural scene."

Momo glanced at the notebook computer that Mother had brought with her, the shell embossed with the MegaHard logo. She'd seen that notebook before.

So Mother had come to see her, but made sure to bring her work too.

"Momo, give me a chance to explain."

"How efficient of you to bring along your work computer! You can use my salon as your presidential suite for the day."

Mother's eyes welled up with tears.

"Let's just celebrate my birthday, Mother."

But Momo had another idea. Involving her scanner.

# 9

At last, Momo opened Mother's notebook.

She now knew the password.

Mother wouldn't wake up anytime soon. She'd drunk quite a bit of spiked apple wine.

Momo couldn't help herself. Her curiosity had gotten the better of her. What had Mother written for twenty years in that carefully guarded notebook of hers?

She'd started scheming the moment she saw the notebook:

Momo volunteered to give Mother a full-body dermal care treatment, but to her surprise, Mother was too shy to take off her clothes. Momo had seen Mother naked back in 2080 when she was ten years old and spied on her with her scanner. At the time, Draupadi was giving Mother a massage, and Mother had seemed totally relaxed. But she didn't want to be naked in front of her daughter? No big deal. Momo would just apply M skin to Mother's hands instead. Momo knew that a workaholic like Mother would have to open her notebook sooner or later. All she had to do was open the notebook and type in her password.

Once Mother had accessed her notebook, Momo handed her a glass of apple wine with a mild intoxicant. Mother drank it and soon fell fast asleep. Then Momo gently bathed Mother's hands in a removal agent and peeled off the M skin. The M skin had recorded Mother's password.

Momo downloaded the data from Mother's M skin to her computer. Each key on Mother's keyboard represented a character and each character corresponded to a place on a digital grid. The computer could easily extrapolate the password.

But the password to Mother's notebook computer was further encrypted with seven character strings.

Seven more passwords? Why go to so much trouble for a notebook? A password comprising seven encrypted character strings was so exponentially complex that even the cleverest sleuth could never decipher it. It would have been impossible to crack the code without Draupadi's scanner and the M skin.

Mother was a valuable company VIP; no wonder an array of antitheft tools had been installed on her notebook. That way if she dropped it in the street, no one could pick it up and snoop inside. She didn't even have to worry about recovering the notebook if she accidentally misplaced it. If it was lost, it was lost. She could just go and buy a new notebook!

Early versions of Mother's notebook computer couldn't actually store any data at all; they functioned primarily as a gateway to communicate with remote data processing centers. People just used their portable device to access data on a remote server. So it was no big deal if you lost your notebook computer back then, because it didn't have the capacity to store sensitive information; the cache was instead stored offsite. Primitive notebook computers just needed to keep intruders from gaining access to these offsite servers. It was a bit like uttering

"Open sesame" to gain access to the cave of treasures in "Ali Baba and the Forty Thieves."

Momo was Ali Baba. She keyed in seven charms and unsealed the portal.

Though Momo knew the story of Ali Baba and the forty thieves, she'd forgotten something: when Ali Baba broke into the undisturbed cave, all hell broke loose.

"Cave" was practically synonymous with "tomb."

The screen of the notebook computer looked like a common roadside ATM. In glowing purple letters it read:

"Please enter your password."

Momo entered the first of the seven strings of characters and was greeted immediately by another screen that read, in tiny indigo letters:

"Please enter the next password."

She entered it. And one after another different-colored prompts appeared, each one slightly smaller than the last. When the tiny red letters appeared on the seventh screen, Momo entered the seventh character string.

The screen went black. Then a few seconds later, two bright-colored boxes appeared.

The box on the left was labeled "Work," and the box on the right was labeled "Private."

Without even thinking, Momo chose the box on the right.

When the screen refreshed again, [she saw] a square-shaped grid divided into nine cells. The cell in the very center of the grid was labeled "Momo."

Naturally Momo went to this cell first.

With trembling fingers, she clicked on it and the screen changed to reveal the following table:

| 2070 年 | 2071 年 | 2072 年 | 2073 年 | 2074 年 |
|---|---|---|---|---|
| 2075 年 | 2076 年 | 2077 年 | 2078 年 | 2079 年 |
| 2080 年 | 2081 年 | 2082 年 | 2083 年 | 2084 年 |
| 2085 年 | 2086 年 | 2087 年 | 2088 年 | 2089 年 |
| 2090 年 | 2091 年 | 2092 年 | 2093 年 | 2094 年 |
| 2095 年 | 2096 年 | 2097 年 | 2098 年 | 2099 年 |
| 2100 年 | 2101 年 | 2102 年 | 2103 年 | 2104 年 |

What did it mean?

The grid was laid out in an orderly fashion, just like Momo's filing system for storing her clients' M skin data.

Were these diary entries that Mother had made for Momo?

Momo selected the cell labeled "2094" with a click of the keyboard.

The following words crept across the screen:

—2094: Momo is twenty-four. "Momo Wins Creative Cosmetics Prize for Asia-Pacific Region."

So Mother actually cared about that?

Another button appeared in the lower right-hand corner of the screen: "View."

View what? Momo clicked on it.

The words on the screen disappeared and were replaced by an audio-visual recording. Worried that the noise might wake Mother, Momo turned the sound off.

Ah, she'd seen all this before! Everything that appeared onscreen, every angle, she remembered perfectly, down to the last detail. It was as if she was watching a historical documentary or a discmovie, only the movie was about her being awarded the Creative Cosmetics Prize for the Asia-Pacific region at twenty-four, the best moment of her life. There she was, standing on the podium with her prizewinning creation by her side, countless eyes trained on her amid the glare of the paparazzi's flashes, the screen sweeping across the crowd like the eye of a camera, Mother missing from the scene. Although Momo had turned the sound off, she could imagine the thunderous applause of the audience. All for her. And Mother was not there.

Did this mean—Mother was there, she was just behind the camera? Had she been recording all this to make a diary for her daughter?

Momo, oh Momo! Did you really think Mother was ignoring you all that time?

You're clearly so important to her!

Momo brushed these thoughts aside and kept watching. Her whole body felt feverish, like she'd been burnt in the scorching heat of the sun.

She exited "2094." And selected "2080."

The screen displayed the words:

—2080: Momo is ten. "Momo's Surgery Is Successful," "Momo Goes to Boarding School."

Momo selected "Momo's Surgery Is Successful" and pressed "View." Yes, it was just as she remembered: the view from where she was lying in an ordinary hospital bed. Through the window a withered leaf fluttered in the breeze. Mother approached her bedside and told her she could leave the hospital.

But this time Mother appeared in the frame . . . so she couldn't have been filming it. Maybe she'd used a fully automatic camera so that she could be in the shot too?

It turned out Mother had been incredibly meticulous in filming many key scenes from Momo's life.

The segment on "Momo's Surgery Is Successful" was too long to view in one sitting, so she exited. She didn't feel up to watching "Momo Goes to Boarding School." She selected 2070 next.

The screen blinked and changed. 2070: "Momo Is Born and Named 'Momo,' as in 'Peach.'"

Fascinating! Mother had even been recording as long ago as Momo's birth.

She clicked "View."

How to describe the blurry image?

Distant, removed, and pearly white like an antique photograph.

Momo saw two faces appear on the screen. They were so far from the camera that she couldn't quite identify them, but she could tell that they were both women. They were strolling hand in hand up a misty hill, happy. When they reached the top of the hill, they stopped beneath a peach tree to eat onigiri rolls wrapped in seaweed, singing folksongs. Here the camera zoomed in. Momo could see that one of the women was Mother. But who was her friend? The frame only showed the other woman's back. The two women continued to talk and laugh, but Mother's friend kept her back to the camera.

Then Momo watched Mother put her friend on her shoulders so she could reach the biggest peach in the tree. The peach was as big as a human skull. Mother looked happy and said something. Here Momo couldn't resist turning the notebook's sound back on because she really wanted to know what Mother was saying. She turned it up just a little—

From the screen Momo heard Mother say (Mother's voice was still the same, it hadn't changed) . . . *There is an ancient Chinese legend according to which "peach splitting"—when you share a peach with a friend—signifies an extraordinary friendship. Let's cut the peach in two, each eat half, and bless our friendship!*

Whereupon the two women went to split the peach with a knife, but as soon as the knife broke the skin, the shrill wail of an infant burst out of the peach: Momo was born.

A bitter smile played across Momo's face. Would such a preposterous fairy tale ever convince the children of today, with their proper sex education? It must be some kind of joke. Surprisingly childish of Mother to turn the story into a melodrama and then include it in her diary.

Onscreen, she saw that the baby's face was ruddy indeed, and sweetly redolent. A peach child. Then Mother's friend spoke. She proposed that they name the girl "Momo." Mother's friend, who was Japanese, explained about the boy born from a peach, Momotaro, and that "peach" was pronounced "momo" in Japanese.

It dawned on Momo that she had heard the Japanese woman's voice before.

She knew that voice. But . . .

Was it really her? Why her? Why hadn't she said anything to Momo?

Mother's friend was none other than Tomie Ito.

Momo was sure of it.


Obviously this documentary about Momo's birth was fake. But why had Tomie played the role of the second woman? So Tomie—one of Momo's oldest clients—and Mother actually knew each other well? In which case, was Tomie's Mother's Day article just some kind of trick she was playing on Momo? No wonder Mother had sent Momo an e-mail as soon as she'd read Tomie's interview. Were Mother and Tomie conspiring to make a fool of Momo? And had Momo fallen for it?

What kind of diary was this, anyway?

How many secrets were still buried within it? It was Momo's life story, and yet she couldn't quite make sense of it. She had to know the truth.

\* \* \*

Momo switched to another period and selected the year 2095.

—2095: Momo is twenty-five. "Momo Establishes Salon Canary," and "Draupadi Pays Momo a Visit."

Now Momo was shaken.

*Draupadi . . . ???* How did Mother know Draupadi had come to see her? Why was there a recording of the visit in Mother's notebook?

Momo selected "Draupadi Pays Momo a Visit" and turned the sound up to 50 percent . . . She couldn't wake Mother, but she had to know.

Momo could barely believe her eyes and ears. Not because of what she saw and heard. But because she knew the whole scene by heart!

It was exactly the way she remembered it . . .

Even the angle of her view of Draupadi's face was the same . . .

There was no static. The audio was perfectly crisp.

. . ."What an exceptional name you've chosen, 'Salon Canary.' I'm sure your technique is just as lovely," commented Draupadi onscreen. "I'm curious—who does 'canary' refer to? What does it mean?" Draupadi wore a sari of violet and indigo and carried a small violin case. "Momo, I haven't seen you in so many years. Do you remember me? Your face is still as pretty as a peach, but it's gotten rosier with age." Draupadi entered the salon, silently put down her violin case, and made herself at home. She was only wearing one loose-fitting purple sari, but when she removed it, there was another deep indigo sari beneath. "I'm wearing too much clothing, aren't I? Do you know why I'm called 'Draupadi'?" Draupadi removed her second layer, third, fourth—cycling through pale blue, green, and then yellow, orange, and red. Finally the red layer disappeared, and she was naked. Draupadi sat naked and plump on the massage table, just as Momo remembered.

Momo watched in awe as the videos precisely replicated her memories.

Momo also noticed something strange. In all of these hyper-realistic documentaries of her, the central figure never once appeared: Momo herself.

Momo hadn't seen herself in any of the recordings.

In the journal of her life, her own face never appeared.

If Mother had filmed all these videos herself, then Mother shouldn't appear in them. But this didn't make sense either, because there was no way Mother could have filmed Draupadi's visit!

Momo had a sick feeling in her stomach. She couldn't help but think of the crude scanner she'd had as a child. It was impossible. Had someone surreptitiously installed a scanner somewhere close by to record Momo's life? And then transferred all the videos to Mother's notebook?

Momo wanted to shake Mother awake and demand an explanation. How could she spy on her own daughter so outrageously? But then she thought better of it. After all, hadn't she just been secretly reading her journal? That counted as spying. Who had the moral high ground here?

If Mother had used a scanner to spy on Momo, then she would have known long ago that Momo used Draupadi's M skin technology to spy on all her clients! But that didn't make sense either—because if Mother knew what Momo was up to, why would she let Momo use M skin on her?

Maybe Mother wasn't using a scanner at all?

Another explanation popped into Momo's head before she could fully understand it: Maybe the sounds and sights recorded in the notebook were not technological recordings at all. Maybe they were what she had actually seen, heard, and experienced in her life. Otherwise how could you explain the perfect match between the framing, colors, and textures of the scenes and her own memories?

Could it be that, just as the words "Open sesame" unlocked the door to the cave of treasures, the notebook computer was the portal to a remote mainframe . . . and that everything that Momo experienced through her senses was transmitted not only to Momo's brain but also to a remote database somewhere? Had the observer become the observed?

Could it be that this world of the senses . . . couldn't be trusted?

Momo couldn't stop her fingers and probed further. She was like that pathetic girl from the fairy tale who put on enchanted red shoes and couldn't stop dancing.

If everything recorded in the notebook derived from her own experiences, Momo thought, then what about her experiences right now, her future experiences? There was an entry for the year 2100 in the notebook. If she pressed "View" for 2101, would she be able to see her future?

First she tried 2100.

—2100. Momo is thirty. "Finger Transplant," "Mother Pays a Visit."

She selected "Mother Pays a Visit."

Whereupon she saw a scene unfold, shot entirely from her point of view:

. . . Mother on the monitor, coming through the door . . . Andy the dog growing agitated . . . Mother entering . . . the dog barking . . . Mother and daughter eating peach cake . . . applying M skin to Mother's hands . . . Mother falling asleep after drinking the wine . . . Momo peeling away the M skin from Mother's hands . . . Momo getting into Mother's portable computer . . . effortlessly entering the seven-tiered password . . .

All the scenes she had just watched flashed by on the screen, identical—the scene from 2094 when Momo won the prize; from 2080 when she was lying in the hospital bed about to be released; finding baby Momo in the peach from 2070; and 2095 when Draupadi came over with the M skin. . . .

She'd finished watching all the recordings of the past. Every detail was exactly as Momo remembered, right down to the angle from which she viewed them as she sat in front of the notebook: no deviation whatsoever. Though there was a slight delay, she (re)experienced everything with a terrifying sense of déja vu . . .

On the computer screen Momo was staring at, there appeared an image of the computer screen that Momo was staring at . . . and inside the screen, another screen, and another . . . infinite nest of images.

Momo watched herself watching herself onscreen, a scene within a scene of her watching herself, and watched the scene within this scene of watching herself onscreen, watching, watching the scene of . . .

The Latin term *ad infinitum*—infinite and endless—flashed through Momo's mind.

The world order only seems intact until it reaches a state of *ad infinitum*. Then it begins to fall apart, known as "deconstruction."

An ancient sage known as Derrida once spoke of "différance," whereby your well-intentioned pursuit of the authenticity of sensory experience only produces endless variations, shifts, and evolutions; the meaning you seek, inconstant and ephemeral, is elusive as a chameleon. "Mise en abyme," they say—no matter how many layers of clothing you fold back, another layer of clothing always lies underneath; every password you enter yields another request for a password; within the darkness of the abyss always lies another abyss.

Momo realized that she couldn't see *anything* anymore, for her subjective understanding of the world had completely and utterly abandoned her.

It was like that day when she at ten years old was forced to go through the gory ritual of surgery—so cold, so cruel—while she lay comatose and utterly defenseless.

In the montage of anaesthetized splintered memories, Momo dreamed again of Andy, her sister. But Andy's body transformed into a canary and flew away, high into the distance. Momo wanted to call her back, but found she couldn't use her voice. So instead she drowned in silence.

# 10

"How do you plan to take care of Momo from now on?" On the scorching red and yellow surface of a certain Asian island nation was a building shaped like the half-transparent eye of a fish. The dome was transparent, yet could block ultraviolet radiation. It was a surface Metro station, and in a few minutes an express shuttle to T City would depart, taking about an hour to reach its destination on the sea floor.

Draupadi sat with Momo's mother at the corner table of a café in the terminal.

"Momo has made great contributions to our organization, and we are extremely grateful for her cooperation," said Draupadi. "If she hadn't snooped and read classified information, we'd keep her on. Fortunately she meant no harm, and she didn't read anything too sensitive, so the boss isn't very concerned."

"So let her come home. She's been with your factory for twenty years now, that's long enough."

"What are your plans when you get back?"

"I'm going to ask Momo what she thinks. See if she prefers a cyborg body or a computer terminal interface. For once in her life she should decide."

In Mother's hands lay a crystal box. The box was equipped with a delicate network of tubes that fed an autonomous life-support system. In the box lay an organ, pink and soft: Momo.

Momo had been separated from her Andy.

At last she would get to go home with her mother.

Momo was ten in 2080. After being hospitalized for three years, she was finally ready to be wheeled into the operating room for the long-awaited, complicated surgery in which thirteen surgeons would simultaneously carve her up as she lay on the operating table. Momo was under a general anaesthetic, so had no idea that her little playmate Andy lay nearby too.

At first the plan was to replace Momo's ruined tissue and organs with Andy's own viscera. Since this Andy was designed to spec as a match for Momo, there was no chance of physical or psychological rejection; this kind of transplant was usually successful. But things didn't go according to plan.

When the thirteen surgeons opened up Momo's body cavity, they discovered it was in even worse shape than initial examinations had suggested. Momo's face, skin, muscles, digestive tract . . . her reproductive system, her circulatory system, her lymphatic system—all had been infected with the LOGO virus, and all would need to be replaced with cyborg organs. For three years in the sterile environment of the hospital ward, they'd been able to slow the spread of the virus, but they couldn't just send her back there and they didn't have a backup plan. She was already under the knife; might as well keep going and finish the operation. The surgeons attached life-support tubes to Momo's prone body and began to extract all the infected parts. In the end, Momo's brain was the only organ to survive. Of Momo's entire body, the only sound part left—her only viable part—was her brain.

And just like that, they transferred Momo's brain into Andy's body. Did that mean Momo was the recipient of Andy's body, or Andy received Momo's brain? Maybe this tricky question of subject versus object wasn't so important. The important question was whether, after her brain was transplanted into Andy's body, Momo could live like a normal little girl.

And the answer was no. A resounding no. The proportion of cyborg organs in the body was too great—or rather, the ratio of human to cyborg organs was too low. Andy's designers had never anticipated that Momo's brain would be the only salvageable organ left in her body; even if they could successfully merge the two, Momo's juvenile brain wouldn't be capable of controlling a cyborg body. In 2080, mainstream biomedicine still couldn't solve this problem. Even if you swapped Andy for the most cutting-edge model cyborg, it would be useless to ten-year-old Momo.

But just as the doctors were on the verge of giving up, worried that Momo's brain would never survive, Draupadi showed up with a startling proposal.

And Mother accepted it. The most important thing was for Momo's brain to survive; everything else was second. They signed a contract.

Draupadi called on Momo several times during Momo's stay in the hospital. She said she was a special representative of ISM Enterprises.

ISM Enterprises was a relatively new company that had acquired considerable social capital and prestige among various corporations and nations of the Pacific Basin. Its business centered on M units—specifically, amphibious combat cyborgs— and it was known for the excellent build quality and maintenance support of its products. You could say ISM was the new century's arms and munitions industry *parvenu*.

Even the name inspired awe. Pronounced in Chinese, for instance, ISM even *sounded* like "Deity." And "ISM" could be found in many of the world's more provocative hegemonic concepts: concepts such as imperial*ism*, colonial*ism*, capital*ism*, fasc*ism*, national*ism*, sex*ism*, heterosex*ism*, rac*ism*, fundamental*ism*, postmodern*ism* . . . and so on. The fact that Draupadi represented ISM was not trivial. So when she showed up unexpectedly at the hospital, the administration dared not protest.

Early on in her visits to Momo, Draupadi seemed to understand that in 2080, state-of-the-art medical treatments could never save her. Draupadi had a unique take on the best use of biotechnology.

There were two main approaches to merging humans and cyborgs. The more common view was that you heal people by just excavating the organs you need from the cyborg and then transplanting them into the human. But the other thought was that you could transplant human organs into cyborgs to make them even more humanlike. Both of these approaches had advantages for the human race and could extend human life, so why renounce the second approach and cling obstinately to an anthropocentric human*ism*? Draupadi argued. Draupadi promised to place Momo's brain in the care of ISM Enterprises; the company's most cutting-edge model cyborg even included a custom compartment designed to hold the human brain.

All this notwithstanding, ISM acknowledged that while this new model of cyborg possessed extremely advanced artificial intelligence, when faced with detail-oriented work it lacked fine motor control—for that you needed a live human brain. But very few people were willing to lend out their brains. So Draupadi had come to the hospital in search of a donor.

In the end Mother signed a lease with Draupadi and loaned Momo's failing brain to ISM.

The contract stipulated that ISM must exhaust every high-tech resource at its disposal to support not only the survival of Momo's brain within its cyborg body but also its healthy development, including its intellectual capacity. In return, ISM would cover all costs, including all the medical expenses Momo had incurred over three years in the hospital.

Such generosity came at the price of a twenty-year lease. Mother gave ISM full custody of Momo's brain for the entire period. If Mother wanted to visit her daughter, she would have to submit an application first, and ISM would not permit Mother to meddle in Momo's reeducation in any way. And Momo's brain would be obliged to work for ISM. At the end of the twenty-year term, both parties could reassess and decide whether or not to renew the lease.

Mother agreed. If there was a chance Momo could live, no matter how slim, she had to follow this one ray of hope.

In the operating room, little Andy's body had no use value and was disposed of as waste. Apart from a few samples to donate for medical research, the remains of Momo's infected organs were also incinerated. And Momo's brain was placed in a special crystal box outfitted with a life-support system, like Snow White in her glass coffin, that Draupadi was to take back to ISM headquarters. But ISM HQ wasn't under the ocean. It was in some remote location on earth's surface.

What could Mother do for Momo? She'd entrusted her daughter to a massive, soulless conglomerate located in an institute on the scorched yellow surface of the earth. She knew that she wouldn't be able to challenge ISM any more than you'd be able to challenge MegaHard, and that she should probably resign herself to her passive position. But she couldn't accept that.

So she decided she would write Momo a diary.

# 11

Momo lacked sense organs, so she had no way of perceiving the world.

But Mother hoped that in Momo's twenty years at ISM she wouldn't think of herself as just a brain, alone and lacking in self-esteem. She wanted Momo to be like any healthy growing girl, with a rich and complex life story.

Her brain should feel longing; read fairy tales; experience sex; have intimate relationships, an education, and a career; have girlfriends, boyfriends, or be single; and even have opinions about her relationship with her mother. Mother worried that Momo's brain would never have the chance to imagine all the things a girl might imagine. So she would imagine them for her. She would stimulate Momo's neurons by writing a diary.

Working in MegaHard's publishing division, it was easy for Mother to order custom discbooks. She wrote one script after another, forwarding them to MegaHard's production department. And one after another, high-production-value laserdisc diaries were created. Mother then dispatched the laserdisc diaries to the surface, care of Draupadi, with the request that ISM play them to Momo, to stimulate her brain and convince her that what she saw in these discbooks were in fact her own memories.

The title of the first laserdisc diary that Mother made was "Momo Is Discharged from the Hospital." The script she wrote was as follows:

## MOMO IS DISCHARGED FROM THE HOSPITAL

**Date:** Sometime in 2080. Momo is ten years old.

**Setting:** A typical single-occupancy hospital ward with a white hospital bed, a window, a breeze blowing in. There is a tree visible through the window. A single leaf hangs from the tree.

**Characters:** Mother and Momo.

**Dialogue:** *Momo awakens to find Mother sitting beside her. Momo notices the open window. A light breeze blows from the window onto Momo's bed.*

MOTHER: Momo, the surgery was a success! You don't have to stay in a sterile hospital room anymore. Now you can stay in a normal ward with a window and watch the leaves.

MOMO: [purposely left blank to allow Momo's brain to reply as it wishes]

MOTHER: And I have more good news for you: Mother has been promoted. I'm not just a run-of-the-mill sales representative anymore. I'm now a marketing director. From now on we're going to be much better off.

MOMO: [left blank]

*The hospital's formal discharge paperwork is completed several days later.*

**Setting:** Same as above.

*Momo lies on the white sheets of a hospital bed. She sees that Mother has carved out time from her busy schedule to take Momo back home, and watches as Mother approaches her in slow motion.*

*Special effect: Mother's eyes are wet.*

MOTHER: Momo, we can go home now. You haven't been home in so very, very long.

Mother sobbed as she wrote this part of the script. But she hurried to finish the laserdisc and send it to the surface. Ootherwise she was sure Momo's brain, all alone at ISM with nothing to think, would feel horribly sad and lonely.

As time went on, Mother set aside time from her sales work to stay up late and cook up scripts for Momo. First she wrote the scenes from Momo's life at boarding school, and then she went back and wrote the scene of Momo's birth: a fairy tale in which she and her old friend Tomie went to the mountains to pick peaches. . . .

She sent all these laserdisc diaries to Momo. Momo never knew the truth—she thought these diary entries were her real life.

In reality, Mother never saw Momo in the entire twenty years she worked on the surface. She couldn't get out of her work at MegaHard, of course, and ISM created endless obstacles when she requested to visit. ISM did accommodate her by producing heavily redacted laserdisc transcripts from Momo's life and thoughts (ISM couldn't hand over *too* much detail of Momo's life and thoughts, since it was a top-secret arms and munitions dealer, after all). Still, it was Momo's diary of sorts, and it was sent down below the sea to T City for Mother to read.

In the disc diaries, all Mother could see was that Momo's brain had been placed into the body of a faceless cyborg worker—faceless because her work didn't require any social interactions with humans. She looked like a common plastic mannequin in a department store, with no distinguishing features apart from a ten-digit serial number engraved on her neck.

From what she could see on the discs, Momo's new body lived out its days locked in an M unit repair shop. The repair shop—which in Momo's mind was a salon built in the shape of an infinity symbol—specialized in precision reinforcement work and was better equipped than most. Momo's job consisted of inspecting M units that had been sent in for repair and restoring their surfaces, applying lubricants, and replacing various components. This was crude work that could normally be handled by a common android, but when it came to the finely calibrated, heavy-duty M units, only a human brain—with its meticulous attention to detail—would suffice. This was where Momo's brain came in. ISM admitted that Momo's case was a preliminary experiment in using the human brain to supplement cyborg labor. But not to worry, ISM told Momo's mother, her brain would come to no harm; after all, doesn't the brain get stronger the more you use it? Wasn't giving her brain lots of exercise better than leaving it locked inside a crystal box?

And yet . . . what a dry and uninteresting job! Mother's heart ached at the thought of it. Mother could only write more disc diaries for Momo, give her more entertaining anecdotes to occupy her, before things got out of control and she became aware of her actual circumstances. Mother also included details about career milestones at MegaHard.

But from the discs of Momo's thoughts that ISM sent her at regular intervals, Mother could tell that Momo never realized she was just a brain laboring to repair androids in a factory on the barren surface. Momo believed her surgery was successful, and that she had gone to boarding school. But Momo's brain was also preoccupied with feelings of loneliness and resented Mother for focusing on her career and neglecting her.

That's so unfair! cried Mother when she viewed the discs. But what could she do? She could do her best to seed Momo's thoughts, but ultimately couldn't control which direction they took.

\* \* \*

Inside a cyborg in an M unit repair factory at ISM headquarters on the earth's surface, three kinds of forces contributed to determining Momo's thoughts.

The first were the fake diaries that Mother sent her.

The second were thoughts implanted by ISM.

And the third were the memories remaining from before Momo's surgery.

These three forces together formed the world as Momo knew it.

For example, Momo believed that she was a dermal care technician. ISM didn't want her to know she was repairing military weapons technology, and so deliberately misled her.

She believed that the M units she worked on were naked human bodies; that when she was performing maintenance on an M unit, she was giving a massage; that when she was applying varnish or restoring the surface of an M unit, she was applying lotion to a naked body; and that her cubicle in the factory workshop was actually her personal dermal care salon.

Momo could be so capricious that Mother became an accomplice: Mother would rather Momo live forever in this fashionable lie than discover the bitter, brutal truth of her circumstances. Since Mother had volunteered her for this difficult task, she furnished Momo's brain with numerous beauty and health care disczines to read, convincing her she was the top dermal care technician in all of T City.

But Momo often distorted and misinterpreted much of the information she received from both Mother and ISM.

For example, Mother's letters mentioned her old friend Tomie Ito—the woman who was like Momo's other mother. But she could never have foreseen that Momo would then read

Tomie Ito's body onto all the M units she worked on sent in by Japanese corporations.

Mother wrote in a disc that she and Draupadi met in the hospital, from which Momo somehow extrapolated a romantic encounter she saw through her secret scanner.

Another time, Momo was performing maintenance on an M unit from America when she accidentally scratched the body. This became the fantasy that she was carving a moon-shaped scar into the neck of a white girl.

When Mother learned of these crazy ideas, she didn't know whether to laugh or cry. But what could she do, expose the reality of the situation?

And then there was the dog. Of course ISM couldn't allow a dog on the factory floor; Andy was actually a "brainwave stabilization device." After many years working for ISM, Momo's brain started to produce static, impacting the quality of her work. When the android was fitted with a new finger, Momo's brain pulsed with anxiety (she still felt traumatized by her own childhood surgery). So ISM installed a "neurosynaptic regulator" in Momo's workshop to soothe and stabilize her brainwaves. ISM insinuated to Momo that this was a little dog given to her by Tomie Ito . . . and Momo believed it.

But ISM's biggest hoax of all was to dupe Momo about the nature of M skin. Because ISM couldn't risk leaking any details of M skin to Mother.

2095 was when Momo believed she opened her own salon, and it was then that Draupadi brought her M skin. It was ISM's latest top-secret product.

Momo believed that M skin stealthily extracted confidential information about her clients. Momo also thought this passion for prying into her clients' personal lives gave her a thrill.

But the clients Momo was treating were not, of course, human—they were combat-ready M unit cyborgs. And applying M skin to the surface of these organisms did indeed provide a method of stealing secrets—it was just that the secrets were not corporeal. They were military secrets. The thrill that Momo's brain experienced in the process was like a candy that ISM provided her—a kind of additional incentive to use M skin. But the biggest candy of all was reserved for ISM.

With every layer of M skin that Momo peeled away, the more of the M unit's experiences she recorded: battle, espionage, training exercises. Every bullet hole or scrape of a meteorite recorded by the M skin was classified military data. Imagine how many laserdiscs' worth of information Momo harvested from these M units. This priceless military intelligence became yet another huge source of revenue for ISM.

In the twenty-first century, the military-industrial complex grew increasingly privatized, while the role of private corporations in military affairs grew increasingly complex, so that no single nation or corporation could supervise every aspect of weapons production. And so ISM emerged as a military supplier specializing in M units, supplying them to many nations and businesses, as well as doing most of their own contract repairs and maintenance work.

Were these nations and corporations concerned that ISM might be stealing their military secrets? Of course they were, and they took precautions. But what they couldn't anticipate was ISM developing M skin—a substance that could easily and covertly record every detail of an M unit's military history without the knowledge of ISM's clients. M skin seemed like just another coat of varnish. Nobody knew the truth except for the highest-ranking figures in ISM.

Even Momo, who most used M skin, didn't understand the nature of the data she was harvesting.

But ISM couldn't have foreseen that, shortly before the end of Momo's twenty-year tenure when her mother would come to the surface to collect her, Momo would decide on her own to misappropriate a password and steal top-secret files from ISM's main servers. Fortunately, Momo only read saved copies of Mother's earlier correspondence—the disc diaries she'd written for Momo—and genuinely had no idea what she'd done. And luckily, Draupadi had been making her rounds of the factory and discovered what was going on just in time to disconnect Momo's conscious mind.

The twenty-year lease Mother had signed was almost expired, and Momo's brain had made great contributions to ISM, so the corporation didn't put up a fight. They just handed Momo's brain back over to Mother, who by this point had been waiting on the surface for some time.

Plans were already in the works for ISM to acquire more human brains to add to the ranks of its workforce. Brains that were younger, more agile, and even easier to control.

For ISM, Momo's brain was just a prototype.

Before Mother got on the express train down to T City, Draupadi said:

"Please don't blame us for taking twenty years of your daughter's life. She lived well with us; her brain activity was very dynamic, and in twenty years she never once suspected she wasn't a complete person. She truly believed she was an ordinary person."

"I know." Mother now wore a more tranquil expression.

"Are you planning to find her a new cyborg body?"

"Not a chance. I don't want her to realize the truth; I'd rather she live forever in her mind, beautiful and whole. Brain-specific life-support systems are easy enough to come by nowadays. Let her stay in the life-support system and rest. I'll find more books for her to read and keep her occupied."

"Momo is a lovely girl," Draupadi finished. "I really like her."

"I know. Thank you."

# 12

S itting in the capsule of the express train, Mother kept stroking the crystal box containing Momo's brain.

As the train pierced downward through the ocean, the waves swelled past, plumes of bubbles breaking against the capsule windows.

*Momo, do you remember the Almodóvar film* High Heels? *After I saw it, I wrote you the story on a laserdisc and sent it to you. Did you read it? In the movie, a mother and daughter are reunited, and at first they have many misunderstandings. But later they come to love each other again. And Bergman's* Autumn Sonata? *That's also about a mother and daughter. I introduced it in a disc diary as well—I remember my heart fell when I watched that film. At the time I didn't know how long I could bear to wait to take you home! I had no choice but to leave you with ISM; they were the only ones who could keep your brain alive. But a twenty-year lease . . . It's really too, too long.*

*There was another film, Visconti's* Death in Venice. *Do you know what Venice is? It was a peculiar city on the surface where there were more canals than streets, and the transport was a kind of small boat called a gondola. Did Venetians live on the mainland or on islands?*

*Hard to say. There were many, many bridges crossing many rivers. When you crossed a bridge, it was like going to a whole different world, so each day Venetians shuttled back and forth among different worlds. The city's carnival was also quite unique: people wore masks of crying faces, even though they felt wild with joy inside.* When I watched Death in Venice, *I got totally absorbed by it, and when the old man, played by Dirk Bogarde, meets a terrible death at the end, I felt like I'd died too. The old man had a daughter he loved dearly, but she died young, and in Venice he becomes totally infatuated with a beautiful young man and follows him all through the canals. Though they never even touch and only exchange vague glances, the old man is happy, despite the signs of disease that have crept up among the liver spots on his face. He doesn't live to achieve substantive, tangible happiness. The young man is just the object of his gaze, hardly even real; so when the old man finally perishes of cholera on the white sands of the shore and closes his eyes for the last time, the beautiful youth vanishes too. And thus the daughter, the father, the young man . . . in the end, aren't they all just lifeless objects? As the notes of* Mahler's Fifth Symphony *swelled mournfully over the credits, my face crumpled in pain.*

*Momo, ah, Momo! Do you know why you're called "Momo"? Long ago I had a friend called Tomie Ito, and we wanted to raise a daughter together to mark our dear friendship. So we set out to get a test-tube baby.*

*Peach trees grew all around the hospital, and some overripe peaches fell right in front of us. Tomie had a sudden inspiration and said, "Ah, so this child really is like Momotaro the Peach Boy in Japanese fairy tales—when we open the test tube, out pops a precious little baby. Let's call her Momo, after 'peach.'" But I replied, "Our little darling baby is a girl; how can she be like Momotaro? Momotaro is a feral boy!" Tomie reflected for a moment and agreed, then added, "Well,*

*even if Momotaro himself wasn't very cute, everyone loves peaches."*
*And that's how you came to be called Momo.*

*It's just that, to our surprise, the hospital gave us a boy—Momo.*
*He even had a little pee-pee. The hospital had made a huge mistake.*
*Tomie and I had to accept it—and just as well, because the little boy*
*was adorable. The bigger problem came later. Not only was our Momo*
*a boy, but his whole body had been infected with a disease that was*
*prevalent at the time, the LOGO virus—it turned out that you'd*
*been infected when you were still in the test tube, but the disease didn't*
*present until you were five years old, and by the time you were seven*
*you had to go stay in the hospital. The hospital said you would need*
*multiple organ transplants and suggested that they might be able to*
*change your sex from male to female during the surgery. They also*
*suggested that we'd better order a small custom cyborg ahead of time,*
*to supply replacement organs. At the time all I could do was nod*
*meekly—if you were going to live, what choice did I have?*

*When I sent you to the hospital, was I making a mistake?*

*I don't know. I was so young back then too. There were so many*
*things I didn't think through clearly. All I knew was that I should*
*take you to the hospital, and then work with all my might to support*
*you. I felt so alone back then, just like you in the hospital—both sleep-*
*ing alone in our rooms.*

*But what about my Japanese friend Tomie Ito? She . . . she left*
*me when you were still very little. Don't ask me why, because I don't*
*have an answer for you. All I know is, I miss her very much. So much*
*that I kept writing her name in the laserdisc diaries, trusting that*
*when you read it, you would imagine her to be your regular client.*
*The truth is, she was a second mother to you.*

The finger Mother was using to stroke the crystal box suddenly
began to twitch. She knew she should get a check-up as soon as
she got back to T City. If she needed a finger transplant, then so

be it; she was an important executive, so MegaHard would cover all her medical expenses.

*Besides sounding like "peach" in Japanese, "Momo" also sounds a lot like the English word "memo," which is a kind of booklet for recording things you need to remember. There are many things you don't need to write down, things that are not easily forgotten. But people still need memos to help them keep track of their memories.*

*Momo, please believe me when I tell you that Mommy really loves you, really really loves you . . .*

# 13

Fog shrouded the city with the criss-crossed canals like a layer of membrane.

Outlines of land and rivers emerged from the gloomy mist.

Momo lay alone in the middle of an arched bridge as she awakened slowly from her reverie.

It was the end of the Carnival of Venice, and the crowd of costumed dancers had long since passed by the bridge. The joyful cacophony of voices had traveled to the outskirts of the city, far from Momo. Momo vaguely recalled that some of the costumed dancers were dressed as vampires, some as the madman Hitler, and some as the sex goddess Marilyn Monroe: with all the men dressed as women, of course. But more people wore the traditional Carnival attire of Venice: harlequin masks with tears of gold and silver, their garish costumes embellished with ornaments like a cuckoo clock or a chip from Intel Computing Corp., or some even with quaintly avant garde rainbow condom balloons.

But what was Momo dressed as?

She stood up, but she wasn't in a hurry to cross to dry land. Instead she leaned her head over to look at her reflection in the river. The still, dead water cooperated, perfectly reflecting Momo's face.

She was also dressed as a harlequin. On her face she wore the most traditional of crying masks, but on her head there was something rather unique. Mounted on the crown of her head was a delicate birdcage, and in the birdcage was a canary. The bird didn't sing, nor did it hop about; it was as though sound asleep in a dark cave of sweet dreams.

The people had all gone far away.

Momo didn't know where she should go. Which bridge should she cross, toward which piazza? Or should she get off the arc of the little bridge, remove her mask, and draw some water to wash her face?

As she hesitated, she heard a familiar voice calling to her.

It was Mother. She was walking toward Momo in slow motion, like in an old movie. In the special effects for this scene, Mother's eyes are wet.

And there was a canary perched on the crown of Mother's head too, also locked in a cage. Meanwhile, the fog lingered over the city's rivers like a fine white membrane.

*Momo, we can go home now,* Mother said. *You haven't been home in so very, very long.*

# PROMISCUOUS LITERACY: TAIPEI PUNK AND THE QUEER FUTURE OF *THE MEMBRANES*

ARI LARISSA HEINRICH

*If a few years from now we all have Apple glasses on, Alexa has a body, and your mother who lives thousands of miles away is here, then the way we walk around a room is going to be governed by ghosts no one else can see.*

—Professor Jeremy Bailenson, quoted in Patricia Marx,
"Taking Virtual Reality for a Test Drive," *The New Yorker*,
December 9, 2019

To contemporary readers of speculative fiction in English, many of the dystopian figures in Ta-wei Chi's 1996 novel—the cyborg laborers and the "heirloom" animals, the radiation-proof combat drones and the powerful media monopolies—could seem familiar. But twenty-five years after its initial publication in Chinese, *The Membranes* still sparkles with originality. The book offers wisdom to spare on identity politics, gender, literacy, technology, social change, and the future. Culminating with a *Matrix*-like plot twist about perception and identity, the novel is in many ways about the act of reading itself, as well as the mind's subjective experience of time and intimacy. In the several hours it takes you to read it, *The Membranes* asks you first to suspend disbelief, and then to reflect on how the experience of literary absorption can impact not only your sense of time but also your sense of self. There are allegorical implications to this device, of course, but there are also personal ones. Who are you before you read the book, and who after?


## HYBRID WORLDS

Of course, context also impacts the subjective experience of reading. What was it like to read *The Membranes* when it first came out a quarter century ago? As noted elsewhere, the lifting of martial law in 1987 unleashed in Taiwan "a massive shockwave in the island's social and cultural life," such that everyday urbanites suddenly gained unprecedented access to a dizzying variety of Japanese, European, and American literature, music, and film.[1] With the cultural tourniquet of martial law released, literary experimentation flourished. As the scholar Fran Martin notes, "During this period there emerged a new literary movement whose authors . . . [worked in] an unprecedentedly wide variety of styles, including realism, surrealism, metafiction, 'psychological literature' . . . and feminist writing," such that "literary culture in this period [began] to include alongside traditionally high cultural literary forms popular forms such as fantasy, mystery, martial arts fiction and science fiction."[2] *The Membranes* lampoons this plurality when it imagines a powerful future business entity called ISM Corporation. Even the name of this corporation "inspires awe," explains the narrator, since the component letters "can be found in many of the world's most provocative hegemonic concepts: concepts such as imperial*ism*, colonial*ism*, capital*ism*, fasc*ism*, national*ism*, sex*ism*, heterosex*ism*, rac*ism*, fundamental*ism*, postmodern*ism* . . . and so on."

In more anecdotal terms, though, many people of the author's generation (including me) recall sensing something in the air back then. I remember Taipei in the late 1980s and early '90s as a chiral node of punk: a place where youth culture seemed to combine a bottomless appetite for foreign popular culture with an unaccustomed freedom from supervision, all without the peculiarly American stigma against literacy that I experienced in punk scenes growing up in the United States.[3] Musically, for example, Taipei in the early 1990s had some of the most authentic punk I'd ever heard, like the all-girl band Ladybug (瓢蟲), who at the beginning of shows in an underground club near the National Normal University would count off with a decorous and even plodding reserve, only to detonate into a punishing wall of sound, to the delight of the mosh pit below.[4] The lesbian author Qiu Miaojin, another queer contemporary, captures some of Taipei's "punk" sensibility in her celebrated *Notes of a Crocodile*, first published in 1994 and recently translated into English; the novel portrays a group of college friends whose sexual and social exploits anticipate contemporary American identity politics by a quarter century. (Consider for example the friends' inspiration to do away with sex-segregated public toilets. "Hey," proposes one of them during an extended conversation about the inadequacy of the gender binary, "we should found a gender-free society and monopolize all the public restrooms!")[5]

But this maverick spirit wasn't restricted to musicians and literature majors. While researching climate change for *The Membranes*, Chi Ta-wei once met a shy young meteorology student who had been kicked out of graduate school. Along with a small group from his cohort at National Taiwan University who belonged to a club known for staging avant-garde art "actions," the meteorology student participated once when, planning for a show at the student union, the group decided to go fossicking for bizarre materials in a local cemetery. (A pharmacy major who knew something about anatomy described the human remains to the group as they extracted them.) What later became known as the "gravediggers incident" was only discovered when an urn containing leg bones was found on university property. It was 1992. "There was a spirit of chaos and curiosity," the meteorology student later explained. "It felt like a free-for-all. A sense among students that we could do anything, try anything, really test the limits." The students were emboldened by a pervasive sense of restlessness in the wake of the lifting of martial law. From the vantage point of the twenty-first century and its signature undifferentiated information overload, it may be hard to grasp just how intense were the emotional and psychological effects of the sudden flood of new ideas, combined with the relative lack of statutory oversight, on a whole generation of youth.

But the kids were alright. Youth of Chi's generation consumed media voraciously, rebelliously, and indiscriminately, their readings and viewings often curated by coincidence. Texts were photocopied freely near universities and shared hand to hand; pirated translations of books from Japan, Europe, and the United States appeared, often unattributed; bootleg CDs of movies with sometimes hilariously interpretive subtitles appeared for sale by street vendors at night markets and city sidewalks; kids flocked to the warrens of tiny serviced screening rooms known as "MTVs," where you could have a beer or a pot of tea in air-conditioned comfort while watching a movie chosen from a thick ring binder of VHS titles. In their consumption of movies, music, and literature, the youth of post-martial law Taipei participated in a kind of promiscuous literacy that in many ways was the antithesis of the present-day Ouroburos of optimized information streams. Nobody could guess what kinds of materials would become available, let alone predict taste, and consumers were obliged to interpret fresh material against what they already knew. It was an inherently creative, cross-platform, and transhistorical reading process. Chi Ta-wei recalls for instance that many university students initially understood the theorist Judith Butler's influential book about gender performativity, *Gender Trouble*, as science fiction (and he suggests, with characteristic mischief, that many still do).[6] Fran Martin notes how "in certain of Taipei's lesbian bars in the mid-1990s you were as likely to hear k. d. lang as accompaniment to your *shaoxing* wine or Kirin beer as you were to hear Hong Kong's Faye Wong or Taiwan's Sandee Chan."[7] Authors and directors from this period drew on sources as diverse as Freudian theory and traditional Chinese texts about feminine virtue, biblical tales about Samson and Delilah, the symbolic language associated with China's Yellow River, the films of Yasujiro Ozu, and magical realism. Qiu Miaojin's writing is so dense with allusions that it can make your head spin, starting with her earliest short stories and only gathering momentum when she studied in Paris under the celebrated feminist thinker Hélène Cixous. Cultural production in this period was a riot of hybridity.[8]

Chi Ta-wei was at the epicenter of the riot. Born in 1972, he read widely as a youth, and then earned both bachelor's and master's degrees from the Department of Foreign Languages and Literatures at the prestigious National Taiwan University, during which time he also translated major works of literature by Italo Calvino and Manuel Puig from English into Chinese. From there he went on to study comparative literature at UCLA, where he earned a doctorate in 2006. During this time Chi also emerged as an award-winning author in his own right. Developing diverse literary styles ranging (as Martin notes) "from fantasy and science fiction to politically engaged vignettes about queer life in contemporary Taiwan," Chi produced multiple collections of stories and essays and edited anthologies of local queer fiction and criticism.[9] *The Membranes*, which won the *United Daily News* Novella Prize in 1995, contains multiple allusions to writers, directors, and philosophers from Almodovar to Bergman, from Shakespeare to Lacan. As Chi notes in the preface to a new edition of *The Membranes*, the book itself "is like a cyborg body . . . made of disparate parts [including] intertextual and extratextual allusions and references, primarily from imported films, literature, theory, art, and music, without which the story simply wouldn't work."[10] As with Qiu Miaojin's work from the same period, the appearance of these many intertextual references in *The Membranes* was not meant to broadcast the author's erudition. Rather, like a primitive hyperlink, it offered readers connection to some of the key source texts that informed its production. Thus Chi's comparison of *The Membranes* with the body of an android is more than just an apt analogy: the novel's many sources, both ambient and direct, included speculative and science fictions obsessed with robots, androids, and cyborgs, ranging from classics by Stanisław Lem and Isaac Asimov, to Ridley Scott's 1982 *Blade Runner* (and other works by, and adaptations of, Philip K. Dick), to William Gibson's 1984 *Neuromancer*. Though back in the 1990s, "the concept of 'android' was still quite fresh," observes Chi, by 2011 "the concepts of 'android,' 'clone,' and 'replicant' [were] ubiquitous." Channeling the scholar Donna Haraway's influential 1985 essay "A Cyborg Manifesto," Chi adds that in any event, androids and cyborgs aren't only the stuff of fiction. People were anyway "already cyborgs," he points out, "outfitted inside and out with artificial components: scaffolds for internal organs, prosthetic limbs, contact lenses, protective talismans procured from temples, back tattoos, the smartphones that never leave our hands."[11] The beauty of reading from diverse cultures, as Chi and his contemporaries demonstrate so exquisitely, is that you can read selectively and then build something entirely fresh, something shockingly undisciplined by the more sclerotic standards of genre.

## THE MEMBRANES

*The Membranes* is a dystopian fable about a young woman living in a dome under the sea in a bleak near future, when climate change and the expansion of the ozone hole have made the earth's surface mostly uninhabitable. Momo prefers to live alone, though at one point she agrees to adopt a dog—a real dog. But even if she weren't naturally a loner, Momo is too busy for romance: she is the most celebrated aesthetician in all of T City, a "dermal care technician" whose clients include some of the most famous figures of the day. We meet Momo when she's thirty years old and about to see her mother, from whom she's been estranged for nearly twenty years.

In this highly internal novel, much of the "action" takes place inside Momo's head as she reflects on her childhood and puzzles over her mother's disaffection from her. Over the course of the book, however, readers gradually discover that things are not as they seem: Momo is not a human after all but a cyborg, and not only is she a cyborg, but the only organic part of her body is her brain, which was the only organ to survive a devastating childhood virus. Nor is Momo in fact a celebrity aesthetician, as she believes. In actuality—her brain providing the fine motor control needed to operate the hands of an android worker body—she spends solitary days in a munitions factory repairing combat droids, paying down a twenty-year lease to the mega-corporation that fronted the money for her expensive childhood surgeries.

Momo's life as a celebrity aesthetician thus turns out to be entirely fabricated, a series of scripts composed by her mother to ease her child's loneliness during her period of indenture to ISM Corporation. Though we readers eventually gain a degree of omniscience about her story, Momo herself never learns the full extent of it. Like breakthrough bleeding, she dreams of combat droids on the scorched surface of the earth or hears fragments of a melody she can't quite place. Eventually Momo gains access to her mother's confidential computer files, where she learns that even her most cherished memories are scripted in minute detail and stored, like movies, in a *mise-en-abyme* of nested archives. Yet while Momo's lived experiences are revealed one after another to be fiction, the reality of her emotions in *The Membranes* is never questioned. Trying to make sense of what she sees, Momo gets caught in a literal spiral, an infinite loop of longing and loss.

## QUEERNESS

As polymorphously perverse as *The Membranes* may be in terms of source and style, it's still possible to classify the book generically. For example, although *The Membranes* is not explicitly "about" queerness per se, it is often cited among a pantheon of works of queer contemporary Taiwan literature. This is partly due to the identity of its author: Chi Ta-wei is one of the best-known authors and writers of queer fiction and criticism in the Chinese-speaking world, recognized not only for his prize-winning fiction—including *The Membranes*—but also for many short stories on a range of topics related to LGBT and queer or *tongzhi* cultures, as well as for his scholarly work in queer and disability studies at National Chengchi University. Chi recently published a full-length, "magisterial" history of *tongzhi* literature in

Taiwan, and he contributes regularly to "discussions about sexuality . . . through his columns in Taiwan's major newspapers and magazines."[12]

But another reason *The Membranes* is sometimes read as queer fiction is that its characters behave queerly, albeit in a matter-of-fact fashion. More than twenty years before Taiwan legalized same-sex marriage, for instance, *The Membranes* presents as quite unremarkable that Momo has two mommies—mommies who commission Momo as a "test-tube" baby and later break up. In a kind of tribute to feminist utopias, Chi eliminates most "male" characters from *The Membranes*, so that the only adult person with a penis we see in the book—a caricature of a gay profligate, a figure who smacks of self-satire—is only referred to indirectly by the sympathetic cyborg whose organs will soon be harvested in his master's service.[13] Though in one memorable episode Momo "plays doctor" with her cyborg organ donor as a child, she never shows a strong interest in partner-oriented sexuality later on, regardless of sex or gender (in fact, she rejects the advances of a classmate in aesthetician school in a rather extreme fashion). Nonetheless, she does demonstrate a somewhat voyeuristic curiosity about the sex lives of her clients once she opens her own practice.

Even the future is queer in *The Membranes*. The narrative does not place much faith in the sanctity of heterosexual reproduction that is so often the bedrock of apocalypse fantasy, where the goal of the propagation of humanity (regularly manifested in the portrayal of the survival of the nuclear family) is taken for granted. *The Membranes* provides neither role models for nor suggestions about the continuation of the human race. Instead, the human race, which has in any event only barely "survived" the effects of climate change, remains hell-bent on destroying itself. *The Membranes* portrays among other things a (social) world of failure, of *non*productivity, and of alienation where—predicting our own moment of internet and gaming addiction—the denizens of T City become so lost in virtual realities that they begin to confuse the real and the fake. A brief but searing passage in this novel from post-martial law Taiwan even queers race (another classic default of post-cold war science fiction is to champion "universal" values while portraying the de facto dominance of white heteropatriarchy). In this scene, whiteness is toppled from its biopolitical pedestal through the depiction of a sun-punished future Los Angeles where powerful, religion-sponsored coalitions of people with higher concentrations of melanin exclude whites from their political calculus. Finally, late in the story we learn that Momo was assigned male at birth, and that until her illness and subsequent surgery between the ages of seven and ten, she'd had a penis—though according to the narrative as we receive it, Momo never liked her penis anyway, and was more than happy to have it removed ("It was just an annoying bit of flesh"). In this way *The Membranes* is also arguably the first work of modern fiction in Chinese to feature a protagonist who is, or could be understood to be, a transgender woman.

## GENDER ON THE BRAIN

Another way to orient the novel in terms of genre is to position it within a long and diverse lineage of works that use the trope of brain transplant as a device for staging critical social commentary. Moving backward in time, this lineage includes not only works as early as Mary Shelley's *Frankenstein; or, The Modern Prometheus*, but also—following Descartes—literary thought experiments featuring the infamous figure of the "brain in a vat," where the device of the isolated brain is used to reverse-engineer

scenarios that can explain the mind/body divide and the difference between subjective experience and the external world. In
Momo's case, we eventually learn that she is *literally* a brain in a
vat (or more precisely, a brain in a life-support-enabled crystal
case): with no way to perceive things directly, Momo's organic
self is totally disconnected from the outside world, which in narrative terms explains both her original anxiety and her inability
to reconcile the narratives she "remembers" about her life with
her growing suspicion that something is a little off. (A structural
punchline of *The Membranes* is that by the end of the story, the
third-person narration that seemed so straightforward at first
suddenly reads more like "stream of consciousness"; when the
only corporeal component of your main character is a brain, narrative is literally all you have left.)

By contrast, consider Robert Heinlein's 1970 science fiction
novel *I Will Fear No Evil*, billed on the cover of my paperback as
"the brilliantly shocking story of the ultimate transplant."[14] In
this narrative, the brain of an extremely rich old man is transplanted into the healthy young body of his beloved secretary, a
woman who has been killed during a mugging in the anarchic
zone beyond the safe enclaves of tremendous wealth in the bal-
kanized world of the book's dystopian future. The bulk of this
very long novel focuses on what it might feel like for a man—a
wealthy white man—to fully occupy the embodied sexuality and
innate "knowing" of a perfect young white woman. Despite epic
reshufflings of, and musings upon, the main character's freshly
invigorated "feminine" libido, however, *I Will Fear No Evil* never
speculates about the "opposite" scenario, e.g., the question
of what it might feel like for a "woman" to occupy a "man's"
body (and to have access to all the social capital that comes with
it). To his credit, Heinlein pushes his brain-in-a-vat thought
experiment in some surprising directions by hypothesizing
(among other things) a future world in which there are at least

six genders; where enlightened men can sleep with men, "no huhu"; and where polyamory is the norm. But despite these adventures, gender and sex are never decoupled ("I never *dreamed* how much *more* it is, to be a woman," reflects the main character to her body's former owner, who remains present in the body even after the brain transplant. "It's our *whole* body"). Instead such an essentialist figuring of embodiment just reinforces the novel's more conservative investment in quasi-eugenic ideologies, expressed here as the continued subordination of women to men and the maintenance of nuclear family values. Women nurture, men provide.

In *The Membranes*, such an embodied understanding of gender is undermined at every turn. Gender is variable, in flux, even an act of will. Momo's two mothers always wanted a girl, so when they go to the hospital to collect their newborn baby, they discover with disappointment that "the hospital had made a huge mistake": They are given a boy. Luckily, the child's mothers are able to love him in spite of this undesirable quality. But when it turns out Momo has the deadly LOGO virus and will need multiple organ transplants to survive, the hospital proposes to change Momo's sex from male to female in the course of the surgeries. The parents accept this second chance and authorize the change.[15] Bodies in *The Membranes* are not hard-wired for gender, regardless of sex, and even Momo (or Momo's central script, at least) expresses little original trauma related to gender. As a child, she compares genitals with her donor cyborg Andy and spies on her mother to find out if she too has a penis, but from the perspective of narrative, the fact that Momo was assigned male at birth is almost incidental, just one among many details of Momo's background to reconcile.

With regard to gender, then, the investment of *The Membranes* is not with nature but with nurture (mostly), and in particular with the superimposition of gender on the sexed body through literal cultural "coding" and scripts. Where the transplanted male brain and the donor female body in *I Will Fear No Evil* eventually engage in extended "interior" dialogues, in *The Membranes* Momo senses a vague residual presence in her cyborg body, but there is no direct confirmation of embodied consciousness. Instead her sex and gender are ultimately fully decoupled from corporeal presence. *The Membranes'* use of the brain-in-a-vat transplant trope thus has less in common with Heinlein's *I Will Fear No Evil* than it does with that other great work of gender-related "science fiction": Judith Butler's *Gender Trouble*, which was already trending among MA programs in Taiwan by the early 1990s.

## THE FUTURE REPEATS ITSELF

In its punk hybridity, *The Membranes* provides an essential counterpoint to the recent vogue for Chinese science fiction in translation, which—while welcome—risks giving the impression that speculative fiction in Chinese appeared *ex machina* in the 2010s, and only in certain registers.[16] For contemporary readers of speculative fiction in translation, *The Membranes* reveals the diversity and originality of Chinese voices exploring queerness, non-reproductivity, and regimes of technocapital, along with a healthy self-reflexivity regarding the reader's own role as a "consumer" of speculative fiction in what scholar Aimee Bahng has called "financial times."[17]

Chi Ta-Wei's generation was at ground zero of an explosion in Taiwan's economy following the lifting of martial law and the expansion of international markets. In addition to its distinctive representations of queerness and gender, *The Membranes* therefore also expresses a profound skepticism about the capitalization of private life and the failed stewardship of privacy in a time when commercial interests suddenly threatened to infiltrate every aspect of life, with everything from omnipresent advertising to emergent surveillance technologies. Needless to say, these concerns resonate strongly with the world in which this English translation now appears. One of the novel's great inventions, for instance, is M skin, the imperceptible film that Momo applies to the bodies of her clients both to protect their skin and to gather biometric data. Unbeknownst to the subject, the M skin tracks everything from a wearer's sleep to heart rate to number of bowel movements ("From their readouts, Momo could tell who had been constipated and when; who'd had gay sex and who'd had straight sex; who liked to get whipped during sex and then have a bottle of Kirin; which Don Juans and Medusas actually spent most of their time masturbating alone in their room . . ."). When a client visits Momo's salon, Momo removes the M skin, downloads its data, and customizes her treatments, gaining an edge in the competitive postozone skincare industry. Demonstrating an awareness of the privacy implications of such tracking technologies, Momo also secures her clients' valuable M skin data behind multiple firewalls. She only succumbs to the temptation to violate someone's privacy when it comes to her mother: at one point she extracts personal data from her mother's M skin, with consequences that cause her whole world, *Matrix*-like, to unravel. Here *The Membranes* foreshadows Momo's use of surveillance technology in a flashback to her childhood, recounting her first experience with a toy "scanner," a minute spy cam that can transmit high-resolution images back to her computer screen. Inventions like M skin and scanners of course directly anticipate today's pervasive culture of fitness trackers and surveillance technologies—devices that promise improvements to individual and collective health, such as contact tracing, even as they expose us to the less philanthropic tendencies of the market. *The Membranes* predicts a time when personal fitness devices and tiny lenses record our every move and our data is harvested for profit, surveillance, and military applications.[18]

But of course the greatest (and most frighteningly prescient) invention of *The Membranes* is the central figure of the novel itself: Momo's brain, hardwired to consume fiction, lonely and sensitive, her intellect harnessed for profit by a giant corporation that pacifies her with illusions of celebrity and a virtual pet dog. In *The Membranes* we see several precursors to contemporary virtual reality, from the manipulation of Momo's life scripts to the competition for audiences among big media conglomerates like MegaHard, where Momo's mother is a director of public relations. A clairvoyant vision of total immersion in virtual reality even extends to war games: according to the new war protocols of *The Membranes*, humans can now watch "the spectacular unending carnage of [cyborg] gladiators battling in barren hellscapes" from "a variety of electronic devices," all from the safety of the ocean floor, where they experience the war games as real. Indeed, *The Membranes*' preoccupation with scripted realities is revealed not only in the work's relentless references to foreign books and movies alongside Momo's constant consumption of "discbooks" but also in the novel's own self-referentiality as the literary *mise-en-abyme* gathers momentum. Even Momo's mother's reality is eventually—ever so gently—undermined.[19] On one hand, you could therefore argue that *The Membranes* is a book about reading itself—about the technologies of reading and absorption in narrative—and in particular about the profound impact of various forms of media consumption on individual identity as it becomes vulnerable to manipulation. As one of the jurors for the *United Daily News* Prize put it, the novel "tells you that your body, your memories, and even the things you say to people, no matter whether you believe them to be benign fictions or retellings, none of them belongs to you anyway. They are all transplants, duplicates, to the point where they can be input or deleted at any time."[20] Yet on the other hand, in the figure of Momo's isolated brain we also find a kernel of something authentic, unchanging: her desire. Whether she is repairing warrior droids in a workshop on the earth's surface or giving clients a massage in her studio, Momo's longing for connection remains a constant. Her central tragedy is that she can never fully act on this desire, since as a walled-off neural organ she can only ever perceive reality as mediated by others, in this case the giant corporation that stands to profit from her unconscious labor (or laboring unconscious). Though Momo has desires of her own, in other words, her consciousness is always already shaped by market forces. In a dark prediction of present dystopias, *The Membranes* gives us a main character who is—literally—intellectual property.

## NOTES

1. https://lareviewofbooks.org/article/consider-the-crocodile-qiu -miaojins-lesbian-bestiary/.

2. Fran Martin, *Situating Sexualities* (Hong Kong: Hong Kong University Press, 2003), 21.

3. American punks in the 1980s sometimes shared in a general pop cultural resistance to acknowledging class difference in the United States while simultaneously fetishizing the class aesthetics of British punk. Without open critiques of class, however, some white American punks of my generation tended to bury our middle-class backgrounds, which sometimes came out as a fetishization of rebellion for rebellion's sake,

unattached to values related to social transformation. I always think fondly of the famous scene in the 1984 cult satire *Repo Man*—a film on "the beginnings of the downfall of American capitalist society"—in which two hapless middle-class punks from Anaheim witness a mysterious radioactive force in the trunk of a stolen Chevy Malibu vaporizing one of their companions. Momentarily at a loss, one of them suggests: "Come on, let's go do some crimes," to which the other famously replies: "Yeah. Let's get sushi . . . and not pay!" http://undersoutherneyes.edpinsent.com/repo-man/, accessed September 29, 2019.

4. Check out https://www.youtube.com/watch?v=CQqbgYS368Y or https://www.youtube.com/watch?v=Gl-LteuGSMg or https://www.youtube.com/watch?v=iS47E8M75t8 or https://www.youtube.com/watch?v=heoVGTqNJTQ. You're welcome!

5. https://lareviewofbooks.org/article/consider-the-crocodile-qiu-miaojins-lesbian-bestiary/.

6. See "Banal Apocalypse," an interview with Ta-wei Chi by Jane Chi Hyun Park, in a special issue on "Queer Sinofuturisms" of *Screen Bodies: The Journal of Embodiment, Media Arts, and Technology* (ed. Ari Larissa Heinrich, Howard Chiang, and Ta-wei Chi) 5, no. 2 (December 2020).

7. Martin, *Situating Sexualities*, 29. But see Martin's entire introduction for discussion of hybridity and the postmodern, and also of the centrality and specificity of the queerness of cultural consumption during this time. The examples I describe here are of course entirely anecdotal, not necessarily representative, or at least, representative in only a limited way.

8. Martin, *Situating Sexualities*, introduction. Again, I highly recommend Martin's book as an excellent introduction to questions of hybridity and postmodernity in queer Taiwan after martial law.

9. You can read another translated story by Chi here: https://www.asymptotejournal.com/special-feature/chi-tawei-a-strangers-id/. See also Martin's anthology of translations, *Angelwings: Contemporary Queer Fiction from Taiwan* (Honolulu: University of Hawaii Press, 2003), including introduction.

10. Chi Ta-Wei 紀大偉。"新版序, "集於 "膜, "聯經出版事業有限公司: 台北, 2011年: 4.

11. See for example Donna Haraway, "A Cyborg Manifesto: Science, Technology, and Socialist-Feminism in the Late Twentieth Century," in *Simians, Cyborgs and Women: The Reinvention of Nature* )New York: Routledge, 1991), 149–181. Chi Ta-Wei 紀大偉。"新版序，" 集於 "膜," 聯經出版事業有限公司: 台北, 2011年: 3.

12. On Chi's scholarly work and in particular his volume on queer history— and on the significance of Chi's use of the term *tongzhi* here—see Howard Chiang's review in English: https://brill.com/view/journals /ijts/1/1/article-p229_229.xml?language=en.

13. In his award acceptance speech for the *United Daily News* Novella Prize, Chi remarks that the book is a work of speculative fiction ["科幻作品"] that centers on the representation of desire between women—a theme too often neglected in speculative and science fictions, he observes—and that, in a kind of tribute to feminist literatures, the story for the most part excludes male characters. "This gesture risked seeming presumptuous, but for me the greater risk lay in the existential question of writing itself: There is no place for safety in writing." Chi Ta-Wei 紀大偉。"書寫的 HIGH 處," 集於 "膜," 聯經出版事業有限公司: 台北, 2011年: 13–14.

14. Robert Heinlein, *I Will Fear No Evil* (New York: G. P. Putnam's Sons [Ace Edition], 1987).

15. Similar themes were taken up later in (for example) the 1997 Andrew Niccol film *Gattaca* and the novel (and movie adaptation) of Kazuo Ishiguro's 2005 novel *Never Let Me Go*.

16. I'm thinking of works like the 2013 *Man with the Compound Eyes* by Wu Mingyi; Liu Cixin's 2014 Hugo award-winning *Three-Body Problem*; and Hao Jingfang's 2015 *Folding Beijing*, also a winner of the Hugo award, to name a few. There are now a number of outstanding secondary materials in English on Chinese science fiction and speculative fiction. See for example: Paola Iovene, *Tales of Future Past: Anticipation and the Ends of Literature in Contemporary China* (Stanford, CA: Stanford University Press, 2014); Angie Chau, "From Nobel to Hugo: Reading Chinese Science Fiction as World Literature," *Modern Chinese Literature and Culture* 30, no. 1 (Spring 2018): 110–135; Nathaniel Isaacson, *Celestial Empire: The Emergence of Chinese Science Fiction* (Middletown, CT: Wesleyan University Press, 2017); and essays by

Mingwei Song such as "Introduction: Does Science Fiction Dream of a Chinese New Wave?" in *The Reincarnated Giant: An Anthology of Twenty-First-Century Science Fiction*, ed. Mingwei Song and Theodore Huters (New York: Columbia University Press, 2018), xi–xxii.

17. "Asian futurism can be trick[y] to fabulate, given science fiction's persistent fascination with techno-Orientalist themes and landscapes. When it comes to futurity, it's not so much that Asians have been written out of it. We've become the sign of it, the backdrop to it, and the style manual for it." Aimee Bahng, *Migrant Futures: Decolonizing Speculation in Financial Times* (Durham, NC: Duke University Press, 2018), 10.

18. See "Banal Apocalypse," an interview with Ta-wei Chi by Jane Chi Hyun Park, in a special issue on "Queer Sinofuturisms" of *Screen Bodies: The Journal of Embodiment, Media Arts, and Technology* (ed. Ari Larissa Heinrich, Howard Chiang, and Ta-wei Chi) 5, no. 2 (December 2020). Chi refers explicitly to M skin as a figure representing "the militarization of skin."

19. On the fascinating history of the brain and specifically the concept of "brainwashing" and its roots in early modern Chinese thought—which here also provides some important historical context for evolutions in Chinese understandings of brain function both biologically and biopolitically—see Ryan Mitchell's "China and the Political Myth of 'Brainwashing,'" https://madeinchinajournal.com/2019/10/08/china-and-the-political-myth-of-brainwashing/.

20. Ta-Wei 紀大偉。"被作者狼狼刺了一刀," 吳念真, 集於 "膜," 聯經出版事業有限公司: 台北, 2011年: 19.

# ACKNOWLEDGMENTS

In working on this translation and in working through my own metanarrative about what is real and what is fiction in surreal times, I owe many debts of gratitude. Translation for me is an interlocutive process, not one person alone with a text but an ongoing, multidimensional conversation and shared effort to find the golden algorithm that can yield the highest percentage of "true" meaning in translation, accounting not only for linguistic fidelity but also, more abstractly, for "tone" in the calculus of mood and flow, of what you sacrifice and what you gain in making certain translation decisions. In this regard first and foremost I must acknowledge the author himself, Ta-wei Chi, for his generous engagement with this translation throughout. I am also grateful to someone I've never met, nor even corresponded with, yet with whom I've had a number of deep conversations: Christopher Schifani, who wrote a master's thesis on Chi's work that included a thoroughly researched and precise translation of this same work. As a lifelong second-language learner of Chinese, I am also indebted to my teacher and friend, Meeiyuan Fann, who has not only provided editorial guidance and intricate, thoughtful linguistic suggestions but also has been a witness to the time and many of the events I've described here, a fellow traveler, and to Fran Martin, who first introduced me to Chi's work. I also owe a debt of gratitude to David Der-wei Wang, Christine Dunbar, and the staff at Columbia University Press for their faith in this project. Finally, I'm also grateful to Jane Chi Hyun Park and Eloise Dowd for their critical input and support, and to AA and Zoey Dawson, two exceptional writers in English, for their expert feedback on form, style, and word choice.